OPERATION STARHAWKS

BOOK FOUR
THE ROSTMA LURE
SEAN DALTON

ACE BOOKS, NEW YORK

This book is an Ace original edition,
and has never been previously published.

THE ROSTMA LURE

An Ace Book / published by arrangement with
the author

PRINTING HISTORY
Ace edition / May 1991

ISBN: 0-441-63580-6

Ace Books are published by The Berkley Publishing Group,
200 Madison Avenue, New York, New York 10016.
The name "ACE" and the "A" logo
are trademarks belonging to Charter Communications, Inc.

PRINTED IN THE UNITED STATES OF AMERICA

10 9 8 7 6 5 4 3 2 1

41 said, "Do you know how to prepare a slave for the marketplace? Your fingerprints are burned off. Body hair is removed. You're dipped in disinfectant that leaves your skin raw. Sometimes you are fed a slow-action poison to guarantee that you will die within a year or two. That keeps customers coming back for more labor.

"Are you ready for that?"

OPERATION STARHAWKS

COMMANDER BRYAN KELLY. The Admiral's son whose early mission ended in disaster. *Sabre* is his chance to redeem himself . . .

DR. ANTOINETTE BEAULIEU. The brilliant but disillusioned ship's medic, she's already been forced out of the service once. She has a lot to prove.

CAESAR SAMMS. The only surviving member of Kelly's first command. He's tough, loyal, and battle-hardened—but his lack of caution can ruin them all . . .

PHILA MOHATSA. The volatile junior operative whose secret past on a frontier planet has trained her in the use of exotic—and illegal—killing tools . . .

OLAF SIGGERSON. An older, more experienced civilian pilot, pressed into service, who rarely agrees with Commander Kelly's judgment.

OPERATIVE 41. The genetically altered half-Salukan, dependable, but cold and impartial—who can be sure where his true alliance lies?

OUOJI. The ship's mascot . . . and perhaps much more.

FULL SPEED AHEAD—
ADVENTURE AWAITS!

Ace Books by Sean Dalton

Operation StarHawks Series

SPACE HAWKS
CODE NAME PEREGRINE
BEYOND THE VOID
THE ROSTMA LURE

DESTINATION: MUTINY
(Coming in September)

PROLOGUE

Cassandra Caliban stood by the observation port of her chartered passenger liner. The port was really a viewscreen that showed her a simulacrum of space, for at time distortion speeds the stars should have been blurred in a kaleidoscope of color. She did not care, for as a land dweller she still marveled at the mysterious beauty of space. At every opportunity she came to gaze out the port. They were four days short of arriving for the Galactic Alliance council meeting.

Her *first* council meeting as the Zoan ambassador.

She shivered with a mixture of pride and nervousness. She and her fellow members of the coalition in favor of joining the Alliance had campaigned long and hard to convince hard-headed, staunchly independent colonists that they needed Alliance protection. If Zoe was to grow and develop, it had to end its isolationist policies.

Well, now Zoe had joined, and it was up to Cassandra—daughter of a timber merchant—to make sure the Alliance Council saw Zoe as something other than a backwater. She knew that Zoe's strategic location between Alliance and Salukan territories made it a planet of importance. That was her primary concern rather than the ballots on the council's agenda.

1

"Practicing your entry-to-the-Alliance speech?" asked a warm, much familiar voice behind her.

Startled from her musings, Cassandra swung away from the port and smiled at the plump, matronly woman who had been her executive secretary for the past five months, and a friend for years.

"Janitte," she said, accepting the steaming cup of tea which Janitte handed her. "Thank you. Actually I was giving myself another pep talk. The closer we get to Earth, the worse my nerves become."

Janitte's broad, homely face creased into a smile. She patted Cassandra's cheek with her blunt hand. "You are Zoe's best," she said. "Failure is not in your stars, my dear."

Cassandra hid her frown by taking a quick sip of tea. She nearly scalded her tongue and set the cup upon a low table. Since her appointment as ambassador, she had acquired an unsought fame among Zoans. Even her staff, as competent and pragmatic as they had to be, were not immune from an esteem for her that was beginning to border upon reverence. It made her uncomfortable and sapped her self-confidence, because she wasn't worthy of adoration. Respect was one thing, but she didn't want to become an icon.

"I brought the specifications for the embassy," said Janitte. "They finally came over the datatron an hour ago, and we requested them a full four months past. Jon and Thessic have sketched in the furniture arrangements. The art collections will just fit. But we wanted your approval before we start numbering the crates in the hold."

Cassandra unrolled the pliable sheet of floor plans. This ship was carrying a valuable collection of Zoan art on loan from various museums and private collectors. It had been her idea to fill the embassy with the epitome of Zoan culture, and the sculptures and paintings had to be placed to the best advantage. She nodded, sighing at the enormity of the tasks ahead of her: council meetings, speeches before a sophisticated and highly critical audience, decorating the embassy, and hosting the first official reception. If she thought about it all at once, she would be overwhelmed.

The ship shuddered violently enough to slop Cassandra's tea over the edge of its cup.

Cassandra exchanged a look with Janitte. "What was that?"

Janitte checked her wrist chron. "According to the captain, we aren't scheduled to come out of time distortion for another—"

The ship shuddered again, nearly throwing Cassandra off her feet. She and Janitte clutched each other for balance, then Cassandra ran to the wall comm system and activated it.

"Ambassador Caliban to captain," she said. "Has the ship malfunctioned?"

Nothing, not even static, answered her. Before she could try again, Janitte gasped. "Cassandra!"

Cassandra turned and saw the secretary pointing at the observation port. Two ships, needle thin and carrying no registration numbers on their scarred hulls, were bearing down upon the liner. Cassandra froze.

"They're pirates," said Janitte. "They have to be. They're after—"

"Don't jump to hysterical conclusions," said Cassandra, although she suspected the same thing. "I'm sure there's a reasonable . . ."

A burst of blinding white light obscured the left ship. For a moment she thought it had exploded, then she realized it was firing at them. The deck lurched beneath her. Cassandra fell to her knees, and gasped at the pain.

Janitte ran to her. "Are you all right?"

But Cassandra shook off Janitte's concern. Scrambling upright, she headed for the door. "I've got to see what's happening," she said.

"Who are they? Why have they attacked us? This ship is not supposed to attract attention. Colonel Nash planned for every contingency."

Cassandra sighed. Obviously he hadn't planned well enough. She decided not to spare Janitte from her worst suspicions. "I think they're Jostics."

Janitte paled and put her hands to her mouth. "Jostics? But they wouldn't dare come this far into Alliance space."

"I think they would dare, and they have." Cassandra frowned. "Stop thinking the Alliance is omnipotent. It's powerful, yes, but it can't protect its members from every single problem."

"Then what good is belonging to it?" retorted Janitte.

Almost at once, however, her expression changed to horrified contrition. "I'm sorry. Please, forget I said that."

Cassandra wished she could forget it. Unfortunately, too many Zoans also believed it. She opened the door. "I've got to go to our captain and make sure he fights back with all he's got."

"Fights?" echoed Janitte, coming after her. "But, Cassandra! Surrender might save our lives. We have diplomatic immunity—"

"Janitte, don't be naive," snapped Cassandra. "Jostics are barbarians. Laws are foreign to them. They won't honor our immunity."

"But surely we—"

"We are carrying five million credits worth of art. The contents of my diplomatic pouch is worth even more than that on the black market. Secure those documents, Janitte. Destroy them if you have to. Hurry!"

Janitte's mouth hung open. She looked as though she might completely panic, but Cassandra couldn't offer her any comfort. They had too many responsibilities. Another jolt flung her against the doorway. She caught herself and hurried out into the corridor without looking back.

The deck remained tilted as though something had gone wrong with the ship's stabilizers. The overhead lights had dimmed as though power had been diverted to other uses. She picked her way carefully, pressing her hand to the wall to keep her balance.

Without warning the ship rocked in the opposite direction, slamming her into the wall with enough force to stun her. She slid to the floor, feeling blackness suck her down. With all the will she possessed, she fought off unconsciousness and climbed back onto her feet.

Keep going, she told herself.

Four crewmembers came running toward her. One of them shouted something at her, waving his arms, but she couldn't make out the words. A circuit box overhead exploded in a shower of sparks that rained down over her. She cringed, staggering back with her arms over her head.

The lights flickered, and in the distance she could hear an alarm blaring. Dimly she wondered why there were no alarms in this part of the ship. Was it to avoid frightening the passengers? Well, she and her staff were the only passengers on this trip, and she was plenty frightened.

Strong hands grabbed her arms and pulled her free of the burning circuits. She found herself looking into the face of the crewman who had shouted at her. He was wearing a clear emergency facemask. His eyes were wide with fear.

"Ambassador!" he shouted, his voice muffled behind the mask. "Hull breach. This way!"

Before she could fully register the meaning of his words, he was running after his companions in the direction she'd come from. She ran willingly with them, unable to remember a single safety procedure. Who paid any attention to the safety drills at the beginning of a flight? Now she regretted her carelessness.

The lights went out completely. She felt air rushing against her face and panicked. If all the oxygen escaped, what chance did she have of reaching an emergency station? What of Janitte, Jon, and Thessic?

"My staff—" she began, but before she could complete her sentence a mask was shoved over her mouth and nose.

She choked, repulsed by the stale odor of oxygen supplementation. Bodies jostled her in the darkness; she felt herself being manhandled through a doorway like a piece of equipment. Someone switched on a hand torch, and she glimpsed blurry faces thrown into stark contrast against the shadows.

They were all crammed into a circular-shaped room too small for the five of them. Two crewmembers wrestled a manual wheel that sealed the door. Another flipped a switch and gave a thumbs up signal.

"We've got air. Three hours worth if we take it easy."

Cassandra realized that the crewman who had helped her had also given her his emergency mask. She jerked it off her face and touched his arm.

"Thank you," she said.

Blood was running down his face from a cut on his forehead. He looked wan and dizzy, and accepted the mask which she handed to him. She glanced around at the others and saw that one was badly burned, suffering with grimaces of pain.

"What happened?" she asked.

"The bridge blew open," said one bitterly. "Those Jostic bastards knew just where to bust us."

"Watch it," said the one with the bleeding cut. He gave a warning jerk of his head toward Cassandra.

"Forget I'm an ambassador," she said impatiently. "We're all in the same fix. My staff needs—"

The crewman clamped his hand on her shoulder and held her where she was. "No," he said and his eyes were dark with determination. "We're in here for as long as we got air. We ain't opening that seal until they come and pry us out. Your people got to take their own chances."

"But—"

"That's it! You keep still and quiet, Ambassador, cause there ain't nothing you can do now, see? It's all gone. The captain, the first, the computers, *everything* blew out into space on that last hit. We've been tractored by now or we'd be spinning out of control. They'll comb this place for whatever they can steal. If we're lucky they'll miss us here in this little hole, but you got to be quiet."

"If you won't," added another, "we'll make you quiet."

Cassandra flinched from the menace in their faces. They were as frightened as she, and desperate. She knew they would carry out their threat if she jeopardized their safety.

"I won't cause trouble," she said quietly. But inside, guilt was already gnawing at her. If she survived and her staff didn't . . .

A tremendous, deafening noise blew the world apart. Cassandra was flung back against her companions in the concussion of the blast. The walls came down on top of them, and she had a confused sensation of fiery heat. She couldn't breathe and her ears were ringing. She seemed to fall forever, and her last conscious thought was dismay that the Jostics had found their hiding place so soon.

Commander Bryan Kelly thrust out his chin in a surreptitious effort to ease the constriction around his throat, but his dress uniform collar remained an iron band that dug in mercilessly. There hadn't been time to have the new uniform altered by a tailor before coming to the wedding. He had arrived straight from the Luna-Earth shuttle terminal, and changed into his black and silver monkey-suit in the cramped restroom of the church. The family pew was already full, and Kelly was sitting farther back on the groom's side, where a plentiful sprinkling of uniforms made him feel slightly less conspicuous. The bride's side was all civilians.

The place was packed with guests, many of them in fashionable holo-gowns that shifted shapes and colors to match the shapes of their wired hair. Twenty-seventh century styles clashed with the thirteenth century architecture.

Most people got married by registering a dated contract with the Tax and Revenue Bureau. Then they usually threw a party for their friends. Kelly's brother Drew, however, had to do things in the traditional family way. The Kellys always stuck to what was old-fashioned, conservative, and correct. So here they all were in a church nearly two thousand years old, its crumbling stone worn by the acid rain of the twenty-second century and now restored and sealed with a glistening protectant. The guests shifted restlessly on the hard wooden pews that didn't automatically conform to their anatomical contours.

It was winter on the European continent and, as far as Kelly could tell, this place wasn't heated. A cold draft blew against his shins, making him shiver. The stained glass windows needed sunshine to awaken them to glory, but the only light came from flickering candles up by the altar. The place smelled of mint, musty cold corners, and beeswax.

The organ music was live, however, and it filled the chilly air with a warmth of tone and volume that no reproduction could match. Kelly shut his eyes, letting his soul follow the soaring notes.

41's elbow brought him down from his communion with Bach. Kelly frowned and leaned closer to his friend for yet another question.

41 had trimmed his long blond mane of hair to barely collar length and braided back its unruly tangle from his eyes. The black and silver dress uniform of a StarHawk almost made him look respectable, but no amount of haircuts and dress uniforms could ever completely mask the alien slant of his topaz eyes or the feral way he watched the other guests. He seemed to have made a complete recovery from being possessed by a Visci on their last mission, but Beaulieu had suggested Kelly bring him along on this trip for some additional R & R. 41 had never been to Earth before, and he hadn't stopped asking questions since he arrived.

"Which is your brother?" he asked now.

Kelly looked ahead at the men filing solemnly in before the altar. All wore the crimson and royal blue of dress Fleet uniforms. Swords gleamed from their belts.

Commodore Andrew Kelly, looking more serious than usual, held his stocky body ramrod stiff. His face was a square, slightly heavier version of Kelly's own, but his hair was brown instead of black. His eyes were a lighter shade of blue. He looked pale.

Kelly grinned in sympathy as he pointed out his brother to 41. He wouldn't want to be in Drew's shoes right now. And yet he found his throat inexplicably choked as Drew looked to the back of the church and suddenly smiled.

Kelly glanced over his shoulder and glimpsed a figure in ancient, yellowed lace moving forward in time with the cadence of the music.

He felt suddenly winded, as he had felt sixteen days ago when he received the gilded, engraved invitation reproduced by datatron. Stiff old Drew—always serious, getting a little pompous as he grew older—did everything by the book and disapproved slightly of his younger brother's escapades in Special Operations. It was hard to imagine Drew in love, much less looking as he did now, while he watched his bride coming forward to him in the most ancient of Earth's traditions. Kelly felt suddenly envious of Drew's happiness.

41 nudged him again. "That chalice upon the altar. What is its purpose? Will he cut her wrists and thus bind her to his clan?"

A woman with fan-shaped hair behind them made a loud shushing sound. Kelly shook his head at 41 and tried not to feel impatient. He wanted to watch this, not provide a running commentary.

"It holds the sacramental wine," he whispered hastily. "No more questions."

41 raised his brows and settled back in stony silence. Kelly looked around, but he was too late. The bride had already passed him with a faint rustle of silk and lace, her perfume wafting delicately after her. Her hair was dark, pinned in a knot at the back of her head. Tendrils were coming down. She stood beside Drew, and they exchanged a look that made Elizabeth Kelly in the front pew dab quickly at her eyes.

The service began, the priest's murmured voice rising and falling, recalling old litanies and vows, bound hearts, sacred promises. Kelly crossed his arms over his chest and gnawed on his lower lip, recalling his own two-year marriage contract a very long time ago, when he was a brash idiot too young to know any better. A five-minute processing at the T & R Bureau, negotiations over the termination date, a fee payment, and it was done. Somehow it had lacked something from the start. He and Disane had shared good times, but when the contract ended they hadn't renewed. It had been a fading apart, neither having much permanent effect upon the other, and a faint feeling of failure somewhere without understanding why.

He frowned. Drew had waited a long time, making their

father despair of any grandchildren to carry on the proud Kelly name, but this looked solid. It was doubtful that Drew and Shani would drift apart at the end of their contract, which would be processed following the ceremony here.

The priest towered over the kneeling couple. "If there is any reason why this man and woman should not be joined in matrimony, let it be said now or—"

Kelly's wrist comm beeped. Startled, he slapped his hand over it, muffling the noise. People craned to stare at him. A couple of Fleet officers nudged each other and grinned. Kelly's cheeks filled with heat. The beeping stopped, and he eased out a sigh of relief.

The priest had been waiting, it seemed, to give any protester a fair chance. "Then in the name of—"

Kelly's wrist comm beeped again. Someone in the crowd snickered. The admiral started to look, then kept his face forward. Drew glanced over his shoulder with a frown.

Longing to hide under the pew, Kelly touched the reception pulse. The beeping stopped. He shot an exasperated look at 41, who smiled.

"You have fifteen seconds to clear before the message begins," said 41.

"Hush!" said the woman behind them.

41 turned on her with a glare that made her blink and draw back.

Kelly put a hand on his arm. "Let's go," he murmured.

With everyone seated, there was no way he and 41 could leave without drawing attention to themselves. Kelly's face burned so fiercely that he was certain it must be as red as Drew's tunic. 41 stalked down the side aisle as though he were striking out across an expanse of tundra. Kelly reminded himself to keep a military posture, and pretended he didn't notice the glances being cast their way.

Once in the vestibule, he pulled the worn, heavy door shut behind them and expelled a heavy sigh.

"Damn. I thought I had it set on silent pulse. This had better be good. Drew won't speak to me for months after this."

41's eyes gleamed with amusement. "It is a needless ritual. She has produced no evidence of her fertility. He has shown no desire to blood bind with her."

"Will you stop acting like a savage?" said Kelly in mock

exasperation. "You're talking about a Boxcan mating ritual, which is nothing you've been raised to expect."

41 shrugged. "I wondered if you would know the difference."

"Anything is better than what Salukans do," said Kelly, aware that 41 didn't like to be reminded of that half of his heritage. "Killing each other is no way to start a life together. I like this ceremony better."

41 frowned. "You need not insult me just because you are embarrassed. You know I do not experience blood burn."

Kelly glanced at him, then dropped his gaze. "I know. You're lucky. It's no fun." He tapped his comm in annoyance. "Come on! If we made fools of ourselves in front of everyone just because of a misrouted signal, I'm going to—"

The comm beeped. "Emergency. Recall priority one. Repeat. Emergency. Recall priority one."

41's comm beeped and began the same message. He and Kelly looked at each other.

"Damn," said Kelly softly. "West knows how far we are from Station 4. Why couldn't he call in another squad? Why us? Why *now*? My mother will—"

"Stop worrying about your family," said 41. "You are not this tense when you are away from them."

Surprised, Kelly stared at him. He laughed ruefully. "I guess I do tend to get uptight when I come home. It's just that we all have to be perfect. Maybe I should be glad we have to go."

The door opened and Drew's honor guard filed through into the vestibule.

"Out of the way please, gentlemen," said one of them. "Bride and groom are coming down the aisle."

Kelly plucked at 41's sleeve, and together they went outside to stand shivering in the pewter twilight. It had started to snow tiny flakes that drifted down upon their hair and shoulders. 41 snorted and slapped his body with his arms to keep warm.

"Kelly, let's go," he said.

"Wait," said Kelly.

"How long? We have orders."

Kelly looked him in the eye. "Since when did you care about orders? I'm not leaving without at least speaking to my family."

41 gave up and wandered about the massive bushes of

ancient boxwood growing in the park surrounding the church. In the distance, ground and air traffic roared in multiple lanes along the boulevard. A shuttle flashed overhead as it ascended through the clouds.

The other guests came out, chattering and laughing. When they were clustered beyond the steps, the honor guard took their places on either side of the steps and drew swords to form an arch. Moments later, Drew and Shani appeared, laughing as they ducked the globules of sly-paint thrown at them.

Most of it hit, leaving a momentary damp stain that quickly dried. In about an hour, vivid colors of every hue would show under artificial lights, thus marking them as newlyweds during their nightclub tour. The bride and groom were supposed to dance at least one dance in every club in Paris or their first child would have pigeon toes. The fact that pigeons were extinct on Earth had not dimmed the custom.

41 stopped prowling through the shrubbery and came back to throw sly-paint. His aim was truest of all the guests, hitting Drew square in the center of his forehead. Kelly burst into laughter and pushed through the crowd of well-wishers to shake his brother's hand.

Drew wiped his face with a resigned air, then grinned indulgently as Kelly kissed Shani. "Beautiful, isn't she?"

"Very," said Kelly.

Shani blushed. She was petite, dark haired and dark eyed. Her voice was soft and melodic, yet Kelly suspected that she would rule Drew with a will of iron.

"Welcome to the family," said Kelly. His gaze went back to Drew, and an awkward silence fell between them.

Drew cleared his throat. "I heard about the Visci maneuver. Congratulations."

"Thank you."

More silence. It had never been easy to talk to Drew. They were too different. Even an occasion like this didn't seem to change that.

"Hey, Drew, Shani! You guys were great. Can you believe this crowd?"

A whirlwind came out of nowhere, jostling Kelly in order to reach the couple. It was J.J., his kid sister, looking spruce and rawboned in her newly commissioned ensign's bars. She threw Kelly a glance of apology, then blinked in recognition.

"Oh, hi, Bryan," she said and immediately turned back to the others. "I can't wait to get to the reception. I wired in the holographs. You won't believe them—"

Kelly stepped back, telling himself he didn't have to be offended. He had ten years on J.J. and he'd never been around her much. Still, he wanted some evidence that she was glad to see him.

"I hear you've been commissioned, J.J.," he began.

She smiled. "Yeah, the *Hamilton*. I ship out next week. Who's the barbarian you brought with you? He's over there talking to Kevalyn now."

Kelly glanced across the crowd to where 41 was towering over Kevalyn. She was smiling. She'd gained some weight and looked better than she had in a while.

"He looks straight out of the fringe colonies. Is he part Salukan?"

Kelly frowned at J.J. "He's a friend," he said.

She shrugged. "Weird friends."

"J.J.—" began Drew in annoyance, but Kelly had had enough.

"I've been recalled, Drew. I have to leave immediately."

Drew frowned and gathered Shani closer to him in open disappointment. "I was hoping we could talk . . . specifically about the admiral. He's—"

"He's probably ready to roast you, Bryan," said J.J. "Was your recall why your comm went off right in the middle of the best part? I thought Father was going to go straight up off his pew."

Kelly glared at her. She was green and cocky, just like any other recent Academy graduate. The Fleet would soon knock some of that out of her. He had a sudden, terrible urge to start the process now by telling her the truth about the admiral. But their father's death at the hands of the Visci remained a fact strictly classified. If Drew was beginning to suspect that the man who stood beside their mother today was a clone, Kelly wasn't going to confirm it.

He moved abruptly away. He had hoped to spend several days with his family, getting reacquainted with them, finding anew what was valuable and important in his life. Maybe it was better that he didn't.

Kevalyn was still talking to 41. Kelly veered toward his

parents. They stood proudly, arms linked, looking handsome together as they always had. Elizabeth Carstairs Kelly, silver streaking her dark hair, her face smooth and unlined despite a life of stress, had recently resigned her position as Earth's Minister of Culture. He hadn't heard if she was going after a new job or just retiring. Now didn't seem to be the time to find out.

The sparkle dimmed from her eyes. "You're leaving? Bryan, how disappointing. I don't suppose they will give you an option on response?"

He shook his head. "It's priority one."

The admiral's keen blue eyes bored into him with annoyance. "Then what the devil are you doing loitering about here? Get to your duty at once!"

Kelly barely kept himself from snapping an involuntary salute. "Yes, sir. I intend to. But it would be rude not to speak to my family before I left, especially to you and Mother."

Elizabeth's calm gaze drank him in. "It's been nearly three years since I've seen you. That's too long."

"I know. Schedules—"

She sighed. "Mine, at least, have stopped. I've retired. I want your father to do the same."

She looked at the admiral, who snorted. Elizabeth's smile grew small and forced. Kelly wanted to take her somewhere private, but time was running out for him.

"Mother—"

"Drew didn't expect you or Kevalyn to make it," she said, making the conversation neutral again.

Frustrated, he had no choice but to accept it. "Do you think Kevalyn is—"

"J.J. has a commission on the *Hamilton*," said the admiral. His voice was gruff, but pride still shone through. "Her captain is an excellent officer. She'll learn a lot there."

"She told me," said Kelly, annoyed that the rocky relationship between his father and Kevalyn had not changed. Kevalyn was worth two J.J.s, but the admiral didn't see it that way. The copy should have been better than the original—more forgiving, more tolerant—but he wasn't.

Elizabeth had to know. How could she not? How had they come to terms with it? Or had they?

Kelly struggled for something to say. He hated small talk.

He wanted to spin out this moment with his mother for as long as possible, yet with the guests swirling around them in a confusion of congratulations and leavetaking, it was hopeless.

41 appeared at his side. "Kelly."

"Coming." Kelly bent to kiss his mother's cheek, inhaling her perfume, matching the softness of her skin to his childhood memories. "Goodbye, Mother."

She touched his face with her hand. "You're too thin. There are new lines in your face. Don't live so hard, Bryan. Don't worry so much over your responsibilities. Despite what your father says, we know just how excellent a commander you are. Don't let it consume you."

He stared into her eyes, stunned by what she'd said. She was rarely maternal and she never dispensed advice unasked. So where had this come from? He started to speak, but her gaze shifted to 41 and instead Kelly found himself making introductions.

"It's good to see you again, 41," said the admiral. He didn't offer to shake hands, much to Kelly's relief. 41 had a strong aversion to the custom, despite his desire to do things the human way.

41 gave him a slight nod, then astonished Kelly by taking Elizabeth's pale hand in his bronzed one. "I regret I cannot eat at your table," he said formally.

She smiled at him. "It is my regret also, 41."

He dropped her hand and stepped away. Kelly said his farewells and followed. He glanced around for Kevalyn, but she had disappeared.

A string of aircabs hovered nearby to take the shivering guests to the reception. Climbing into one behind 41, Kelly shoved his IDent card into the slot and it lifted.

Its synthesized voice asked, "Destination?"

"Earth-Luna shuttle terminal," said Kelly.

The cab wheeled about and slipped into a middle air lane. As usual, Parisian traffic went about five times too fast for its amount of congestion.

Trusting the cab's computer to get them through alive, Kelly glanced at 41 sitting beside him. "You shook my mother's hand."

41 stared out the window at a holograph ad swirling at the twelfth-story level. He didn't answer.

"I thought you never shook hands," persisted Kelly. "Don't you have a superstition about it?"

41 met his gaze then. "She would never rob my soul," he said with simple finality.

"Oh."

"I am glad to leave," said 41. "It is strange to be with so many fools. The noise was also unpleasant."

"What noise?" Kelly frowned. "You mean Bach? That's the most sublime music ever composed in all of Earth's history. Its precision and—"

"It was too loud," said 41. "I could not hear anything else."

"You aren't supposed to."

41 shrugged. "It is a good way to get killed."

Kelly started to reply, then stopped himself. 41's origins were mostly obscure, but he had spent his life as a slave, mercenary, and Hawk, in that order. Normal family life was foreign to him. It made sense that he wouldn't understand that this was a safe situation where he didn't have to maintain alertness.

Too much fighting could do that to any man, isolate him and warp him until he couldn't relate at all to the gentle, controlled civilization found here on Earth.

Kelly frowned in a sudden decision and leaned forward to speak to the cab. "Change destination. Go to the nearest communications center."

"Acknowledged," it replied, and they shifted course.

"What are you doing?" asked 41.

"Figuring out a way to stay," said Kelly. "This is ridiculous. We're on leave. The squad is scattered across two or three quadrants. We don't even have a ship yet. West can get someone else for this job."

"He would know that before he recalled us," said 41.

Kelly scowled at him. "Don't be so damned logical. I'm going to try."

Paris Communications Central was a cavernous facility thronged with travelers, bureaucrats, local inhabitants, school-children, and diplomatic couriers. With 41 following, Kelly elbowed his way through the crowd, many of whom were knotted at counters, gesturing and arguing. Apparently there had been a shutdown of Universal Starline, a large civilian carrier, with all flights cancelled from the Luna spaceport, and people were stranded.

They had also jammed the communications lines. Kelly glanced around, and managed to squeeze through the congestion to a desk. The bored operator on duty was Boxcan, with the typical gruff manners of her species.

Kelly pulled out his AIA IDent card. "Commander Kelly. I want to link onto a closed, coded Intelligence line. It's a priority transmission."

The operator's manner changed at once to one both courteous and helpful. She unlocked the access leading behind her desk and pointed to a door behind her. "Yes, sir. If you will step into one of the private cubicles, I'll have that call routed at once to you."

The door led to a short corridor lined with booths that sealed for secured communications exchanges. Two individuals wearing the stripes of the diplomatic corps had booths. Kelly took the last one in line away from them and secured himself inside.

The air was stuffy and poorly circulated. The seat's cushioning had lost most of its foam and sported ancient coffee stains. As soon as Kelly gingerly sat down, a green light began flashing in front of him. The smooth, pressure-sensitive screen came to life.

"Commander Kelly?" asked a synthesized voice.

Kelly pressed his thumb to the screen for a print reading. "Ready," he said.

"Prepare all data for security scan."

Kelly inserted his IDent card into the proper slot. A cursor began to flash in the center of the screen. He bent forward and focused his left eye on it within a distance of approximately eight centimeters.

The retina scan was brief and competent. He disliked them, for they always left his eye feeling slightly irritated and scratchy.

The green light flashed again. "Security scan approved. Standby for transmission. Lag time will be nine minutes."

Kelly frowned at that. It meant he would get orders, not conversation. Nine minutes was an awkward wait for an answer to every statement.

The hissing crackle indicating a long-range space transmission came over the speakers.

"Commodore West speaking to Commander Kelly. Status upgraded to active duty. All leaves and shore privileges cancelled. Proceed to Tanner Nine Tanner Nine. Code 0054. Repeat. Code 0054."

In the slight pause that followed, Kelly frowned in dismay. Code 0054 was a trigger word used to activate the microscopic receiver attached to his translator implant located in the mastoid bone behind his left ear. The soft beeps and blips of machine code began transmitting, bringing on the slight buzz of a headache. Any civilian-operated communications center could be accessed, no matter how many scramblers they claimed they had on the lines. The receiver enabled him to accept coded, highly classified messages on channels such as this, with deciphering provided directly to him by his own translator.

He frowned as it was fed to him: ". . . Zoan Ambassador Cassandra Caliban abducted . . . Zoe wants recovery . . . threatening secession from Alliance . . . traced to Kenszana . . . report to Tanner Nine Tanner Nine . . . priority one."

The coded transmission ended. A soft beep signalled cancelled access to the line. The screen darkened.

Kelly leaned back against the wall, rubbing his temples and feeling drained. He hated augmentation, hated how the lab people kept tinkering with the Hawks, upgrading their implants and pushing for more direct access. If the lab people had their way, all the StarHawks would be walking sets of wire, complete with jacks, needing only a place to plug in.

Kelly shuddered. "Damn," he said aloud.

Pushing himself to his feet, he left the booth. 41 was leaning against the wall. When he saw Kelly's expression he straightened.

"I told you West would not allow us to stay."

"Not even a conversation with him," said Kelly in frustration. "Just orders."

He rubbed his temple, waiting for his headache to go away.

"You got a jacked-in report?" asked 41.

Kelly grunted.

41 hissed in fierce sympathy. "One day I shall walk into the lab and augment them with this." He pulled out his prong and

snapped out all three blades. "We are men, not machines. Where do we go, Kelly?"

"Who knows? I've got the coordinates. We'll have to check them on a star map. Somewhere near Kenszana, wherever that is."

41's brows shot up. "I know it. A bad place, Kelly. A source for rostma."

Kelly stared at him, his eyes widening. Rostma was one of the most vicious of the illegal drugs. Addiction was severe and nearly impossible to reverse. People took it out of a mistaken belief that it made them telepathic. It did affect the pineal gland of the brain, but the usual effect was to progressively explode brain cells. Death was the eventual result.

"If it's a rostma source," said Kelly slowly, "that means Kenszana is a noncompliance planet. Independent and no laws."

41 sighed. "There is much money in dealing rostma. When major money is involved, the cartels are powerful. I do not recommend we go to Kenszana."

"I think we're going to have to, whether we want to or not. We have some important people to rescue."

"How important?" asked 41. "Sometimes it is better to cut losses."

"You really don't want this action, do you?" Kelly frowned and decided to probe. "Have you dealt rostma? Do you know anyone in these cartels?"

A cold distance entered 41's eyes. "I know some of them. They do not know me. I will not give the mission away."

"I wasn't implying that you would," retorted Kelly. "I'm not accusing you of anything, 41. I just want all the information possible. If we have to go in there after these people, we need every advantage we can find."

"Understood," said 41, but the expression in his eyes did not lighten.

Kelly tapped his arm. "Let's go. We have a flight to catch."

2

Tanner Nine Tanner Nine turned out to be a modest docklink station on the way to nowhere. Small and operated by droids, it rotated in its tiny orbital path on the edge of the Carean Drift. The Drift itself was of little interest to scientists, being mainly a dust cloud from a novaed sun, with a lot of asteroids and rubble cluttered together. It was a pain to navigate around, but most traffic in this sector consisted of ore freighters or cargo flats towed by robot ships that weren't in any hurry. The station served as a fueling source and a connection between commercial space flights.

The last civilian ship-to-station shuttle of the day bottled into its docklink forty-eight minutes behind schedule. It carried nearly double its full complement of thirty passengers, most of whom needed a sonic shower. Not only was every narrow seat filled elbow to elbow, but passengers stood crammed in the center aisle in violation of safety regulations. A steward in a shabby uniform stood beside the hatchway and shouted disembarkation instructions to which no one listened.

41 touched his arm. "Kelly."

Kelly obediently turned his head and saw 41 pointing out the tiny port. He leaned over to peer through it and saw a sleek vessel orbiting the station. The ship was a beauty that made his throat tighten with admiration. He'd never seen anything of her configuration before, but the rakish slope of her lines had a grace and power that could only come from Minza. The Minzanese shipwrights were the best in the galaxy. They also commanded the highest prices; few individuals could afford a ship like this one. But the Allied Intelligence Agency could.

Kelly's fingers dug into the worn armrest. "41," he breathed, letting himself hope. "Did you see a registry number?"

"No. But I think—"

41 hesitated, and his yellow eyes met Kelly's blue ones.

"She's ours?" whispered Kelly.

The corner of 41's mouth curved into a smile that matched the leap of excitement within Kelly. "Has to be."

"If she is, the wait was worth it," said Kelly. "Look at her size. She's twice as big as the *Valiant*, bigger than anything any other squad has. Have you seen that design before?"

"No."

"Neither have I. She must be something entirely new. She looks like—"

One of the standing passengers digging into an overhead locker dropped his duffel onto Kelly's back. The duffel was heavy, as though it was full of ore samples, and its impact hurt. Kelly turned on the man, who was wearing a mining company logo on his coveralls.

"Sorry," said the man, making the word an insult. "I thought StarHawks wore armor under those fancy suits."

Kelly put a quick damper on his temper. For some reason it was considered a coup for a civilian to pick a fight with a StarHawk and win. Standing orders for every Hawk operative and officer was to avoid such fights.

Kelly forced a smile to his lips. "Well, we don't. Here." He tossed the duffel at the engineer, who caught it with visible disappointment.

A sharp jolt signifying docklink distracted the man. All the seated passengers surged to their feet and tried to force themselves into the aisle, despite the fact that it was solidly packed with people of several species and temper levels. Kelly had thought his aisle seat would allow him to get off more quickly, but there wasn't a chance of going anywhere.

A fight broke out near the hatchway, which the steward tried in vain to quell. Someone knocked the man sprawling and tried to unlock the hatchway. But he got the numerical sequence wrong, and the other passengers shouted in anger.

More fights broke out. Kelly stood up, only to jump back against 41 to avoid being struck by a flailing fist.

"We're going to miss our connection!" shouted someone.

"Yeah, who ain't on this crapshoot line."

"Let us off! Let us off!"

Kelly exchanged a glance with 41. "This is absurd."

The steward climbed shakily to his feet. "No one gets off until you all sit down!"

"To hell with you!"

The steward glared at them. "I won't open the hatch if you don't calm down. There will be order here! If you don't like the service, take another line."

"There isn't one!"

The steward smirked. "Exactly. Now, all of you step back."

But Kelly had had enough. Jerking his head at 41, he boosted himself to the back of the seat ahead of him and crawled forward from seat to seat. The other passengers shouted and jeered. One man tried to get ahead of Kelly, but 41 tossed him to the floor.

Reaching the steward, Kelly gestured. "Open the hatch before you have a riot."

"Oh, yeah? You don't have any authority on this vessel—"

He broke off with a yelp as Kelly gripped the front of his tunic and twisted it.

"I *do* have authority," said Kelly very softly. "And you are *this* close to being charged with obstructing a Special Operations officer in the line of duty. 41."

41 hit the correct sequence of lock codes for crafts of this make and age. The depressurization light came on. The passengers cheered.

Air hissed as the seal loosened. The hatch opened, and Kelly and 41 ducked out, leaving the passengers to fend for themselves.

They strode along a short connection tunnel with an airlock at the end. An attendant droid scanned their IDent cards and cycled them through the security checks with manual override of the arms possession alarm.

Beyond the checkpoint, a stocky figure with flaming red hair stood waiting. "Yo, boss!" he called out cheerfully. "Long time no look at. Ain't tourist class wonderful?"

Kelly tugged at his rumpled uniform and ran a quick hand through his hair. "Not really. I haven't traveled bottom class civilian transport in a long time. It didn't used to be this bad."

"It didn't used to be deregulated. This way, gents."

Pointing, Caesar started down a corridor in the opposite direction from that which most of the other passengers were taking. 41 and Kelly fell into step with him.

"Did you see the ship as you came in?" asked Caesar. "Ain't she a beaut?"

Kelly grinned. "We saw her. She's the best-looking ship I've ever seen."

"Siggerson's died of ecstasy. And, gee, boss, I get my own room now. No more sharing those crackerbox quarters." Caesar's green eyes took on an unholy gleam. "I even have space to set up my own lab. Beaulieu won't let me in hers."

"No explosive experiments!" said Kelly in sharp alarm. "We've got to take good care of this ship. West will probably never give us another one if anything happens—"

Caesar raised both hands. "Whoa, boss. It was your decision to blow up the *Valiant*."

Kelly frowned and Caesar went on hastily, "You know, I never did like that excuse for a hold. This one's got room enough for three squads. More than what we need. I figure I can talk Phila into wiring in a holo—"

"Belay that," said Kelly impatiently. "What's her speed? How much firepower does she have? How many—"

"Excuse me, boss. Wait right here."

Caesar dashed into a shop that looked as though it sold everything from bar drinks to souvenirs. Kelly glimpsed a garish sign advertising space rubble as GENUINE STAR CRYSTALS—CARRY A LITTLE SOLAR FLARE IN YOUR POCKET.

Kelly glanced at 41 and shook his head. His long legs were cramped and stiff from sitting. He wanted to eat and take a shower.

Caesar came running out of the shop with a Hobari dancer in his arms. About a meter tall and obscenely female, it had been switched on and was shimmering and undulating within the narrow forcefield that limited its holographic projection. Gold sparkles and bursts of irridescent light obscured some of the things the Hobari was doing, but not enough.

Kelly stared a moment in spite of himself, then glanced quickly up and down the corridor. Someone in the distance was approaching.

"Turn it off," said Kelly. "Hurry. Don't you have a case to put it in?"

"Nope. Cut-rate prices," said Caesar, grinning with pride. "I've wanted one of these for years. And this is an advanced model. Obviously black market, but—"

"It's also illegal to operate one in public," muttered Kelly, his ears burning as he heard the approaching footsteps become louder. "Turn it off before we're all arrested on pornography charges."

"Ah, boss," said Caesar in disappointment. "No one on this dump cares."

"Is this a functional holo?" asked 41.

"Nope," said Caesar. The tiny starbursts around the dancer reflected in his green eyes. He began to grin broadly. "Now that's a thought. Maybe we could—"

"Off," said Kelly, reaching for it. "Now."

Caesar stepped back to keep him from touching it, but he did cancel the projection. The Hobari and her gyrations vanished, leaving a plain, oval box in Caesar's hands.

"Commander Kelly?"

Kelly turned to face the man. He was chunky of build, with a square powerful body and a head balanced on a short bulge of a neck. Human, but not old earthstock. Colonists could never seem to pass for anything else. The man wore drab green coveralls with two gold stripes on his left sleeve and a discreet brass pin on his collar. Kelly made a lightning guess.

"Yes, I'm Kelly," he said, extending his hand military fashion. "And you represent Zoe."

"Colonel Nash. Zoan Security." He didn't shake hands. His voice was as unpleasant as a rasp on metal. He didn't just look at Kelly; he stabbed at Kelly with his eyes, as though to make accusations or to knock out answers. "It's about time you arrived for your briefing. Every moment of delay could mean death for the ambassador and her party."

Kelly wasn't in the habit of making excuses for himself. He

didn't do so now. Commodore West had no business letting a colonial in on this operation.

"I understand the need for hurry," Kelly said. "Just as soon as we're aboard the—" He blinked, realizing with embarrassment that he didn't know the new ship's name. "—the ship, the briefing can—"

"No, Commander. It will take place now. Please follow me."

Nash stalked ahead of them, moving to where the corridor dead-ended.

Kelly looked at Caesar. "What is he doing here? Advisory capacity? Or has West let the Zoans take charge?"

Caesar looked blank. "We just got here about two hours ago. Our orders were to rendezvous with you at these coordinates. Nash didn't come with us."

"Commander?"

Nash had stopped and was glaring back at them. It was a good intimidation game to use on a greenhorn, but Kelly refused to be rattled. He joined Nash, with Caesar and 41 following in silence.

There was nothing at this end of the corridor except a narrow door marked NO ENTRY. Nash put his fingertips against the heat sensitive latch. The door scanned his prints, unlocked, and slid open. Nash stopped in the doorway. His eyes bored into Kelly.

"You'll have to pass the same security scan after I go through. Your men aren't necessary. This is strictly a need-to-know operation."

The door slid shut between him and Kelly. Despite his intentions to keep his temper, Kelly felt as though flashpoint had been ignited. He frowned at the door and longed to tell Nash where to take his briefing.

Caesar loosed a low whistle.

41 said, "Shall I teach him Hawks do not take orders from his kind?"

"No," said Kelly, swallowing his anger. He stepped away from the door. "Caesar, what frequency is the ship's comm set on?"

"Oh," said Caesar. "I forgot. Here." Handing his Hobari projector to 41, he dug into the baggy pockets of his uniform. Only Caesar could stretch out the cut of a perfectly tailored tunic. "These are for you." He handed over two wristbands fashioned of sleek, pewter-gray graphite which weighed almost nothing. "Comm and teleport frequencies preset."

Kelly switched on his immediately. "Kelly to—" He stopped himself with a quick frown. "What's the name of our ship?"

"The *Sabre*."

"Kelly to *Sabre*. Come in, please."

The response was immediate. Siggerson's laconic voice sounded as clear as though he were standing beside them in the corridor. There was none of the usual station communications jumble causing static.

"Any messages to me from West?" asked Kelly.

"No."

Kelly swore to himself.

"When are you coming aboard?" asked Siggerson. "This ship is phenomenal—"

"I'm eager to inspect her," said Kelly. "But I've got a briefing first. Will inform you when we're ready for teleport. Kelly out."

Caesar and 41 stared at him. Caesar said, "Just give Nash's butt a good kick. Do we go back to the ship or wait out here?"

"Neither," said Kelly. He pressed his hand on the door lock and let it scan his prints. As soon as the lock disengaged and the door slid open, Kelly waved 41 and Caesar in ahead of him.

It was a VIP lounge fitted out with uncomfortable looking chairs bolted in a row down the center of the floor. Yellow walls and a laser-green carpet swore at each other. A jagged stripe of maroon gashed the entry and exit doors with an emblem Kelly did not recognize. Vid-boxes that could be rented to while away waiting times between flights floated near the ceiling on tiny grav-flats. A large chron on the wall was set to station time, which made it useless to a traveler.

On a table an unappetizing spread of unidentifiable fruit, sandwiches sealed in foil pouches, and soggy *pamishes* waited beneath a preservation film tinted a horrible pink. A pair of steel urns provided a choice of tepid coffee or glout-water. Nash was filling a disposable cup when they walked in.

He glanced up and anger darkened his face.

"I want them in," said Kelly before Nash could speak.

"I told you this is strictly a need-to-know operation—"

"Hawks don't work that way," said Kelly. "Shall we get started? You did say time is short."

Nash glared at him. Kelly glanced around at the lounge and tried not to wince.

"I hope this room is secured. Caesar, why don't you check it?"

"Right, boss." Caesar produced a hand scanner and switched it on. The feedback emitted a shrill whine. He shut off the scanner hastily. "Whew! If they had any more subsonic white noise oscillating in here, the wall bolts would be vibrating."

"Of course this room is secure," said Nash. His voice was quiet but furious. "I'm neither an amateur nor a fool."

"Fine," said Kelly. "I know that Jostic pirates grabbed your ambassador to the Alliance enroute to Earth. She's been traced to Kenszana, which is a genuine hellhole in addition to being a noncompliance planet outside Alliance jurisdiction."

Nash breathed hard for a moment, but finally he said, "Ambassador Caliban and her staff—"

"How many on the staff?" broke in 41.

Nash's eyes snapped to him, then back to Kelly. "I cannot condone interruptions—"

"Then get on with it," said Kelly without sympathy. "Our orders are to rescue those people. We'll do that if it's at all possible. But we don't need any injured pride, ego, and arrogance getting in the way of us doing our job. All right? Who's her staff?"

A vein swelled upon Nash's forehead and began to throb beneath the skin. "Janitte Krensky, the secretary—"

"You got vids of these people?" broke in Caesar.

Nash controlled himself with a visible effort. "Yes. If you will allow me to explain matters in my own way."

"I'm sorry," said Kelly, "but I don't think a formal presentation is necessary." He called down one of the floating vid-boxes. "Is your hard data compatible with this system?"

Wordlessly Nash handed over a small disk. Kelly inserted it into the vid-box and waited for the screen static to clear. Behind them, 41 tore open the preservative film over the food and began to eat a sandwich.

"41," said Kelly without glancing at him," get over here and watch this."

A face filled the small screen. As grainy and poor as the production quality was, it showed them a face of such beauty that Kelly did a double take. A sensation of heat trickled through his veins, and for a moment he forgot about breathing.

"Cassandra Caliban," said Nash. "One of the most able political leaders Zoe has ever produced since gaining independence."

He said other things, but Kelly stopped listening. Everything faded around him but her wide-spaced eyes, tilted ever so slightly. He couldn't determine their color. Gray or perhaps green. Intelligence and compassion glowed in their depths. The alertness in the tilt of her head and the directness of her gaze spoke of a willingness to listen and to challenge. As for the exquisite molding of her cheekbones and the lustrous, mahogany-hued hair spilling over her shoulders . . .

"She is very important to the Zoan people," said Nash, his harsh voice bringing Kelly back to reality. "They would pay any amount of ransom for her return, but no ransom has been asked. We do not understand the intentions of these Jostics."

Kelly frowned. "Kenszana is not a Jostic base. As far as we know, the Jostics have not made an alliance with the drug cartel which runs the planet. How was the ambassador traced there? Homing devices?"

"Yes. Subcutaneous transponder implants for her and each of her staff. They cease transmitting if the wearer dies." Nash swallowed. "Thus far, all are operating."

"Labor," said 41.

Kelly glanced at him and nodded. "Exactly what I was thinking. It's very likely that the raiders sold your people into the labor force on Kenszana. I'm no expert on the harvesting of rostma, but it has to be done by hand rather than machine."

"Rostma trees grow in shallow water," said 41, his gaze on no one in particular. "The roots have to be cut under water and kept wet to preserve their potency. The work is very hard. Labor replacements are in constant demand."

Nash paled. "You must act at once. It is the responsibility of the Alliance to rescue her—all of them! The Jostics have never bothered us until we let the Alliance talk us into joining. Now we must fight off raids constantly. Selling Cassandra Caliban into slavery is another retaliation. You must rescue her *and* destroy the Jostics."

"That's a laugh," said Caesar caustically. "Everyone in the Alliance has been hunting down Jostics for years. You might as well demand that we change the configuration of the galaxy while we're at it."

"Caesar," said Kelly.

"Aw, boss. This guy's a real wide-eyed wonder. He's one of those little backwater rays of joy who scream about Alliance imperialism one moment and come whining for help the next."

"*Caesar*—"

Nash hit Caesar with one powerful punch that knocked him sprawling. Before Kelly could react, 41 tossed aside his sandwich and tackled Nash, toppling him backwards over the row of chairs to crash hard on the floor. 41 got in several dirty punches before Kelly managed to seize him by the collar and the arm to drag him off the Zoan.

Snarling, 41 twisted free. His yellow eyes gleamed savagely.

Kelly glared at him but didn't trust himself to deliver a reasonable reprimand at that moment. What was threatening to become a nasty political incident just got worse. He pointed at Caesar, who was trying dazedly to sit up.

"Go help Caesar."

41's eyes narrowed to slits at Kelly's tone. But he obeyed.

Kelly swore to himself and crouched beside Nash. The man was out cold and his left leg was twisted unnaturally beneath him. In just a few seconds, 41 had done a lot of damage.

Damage which Kelly would have to mend. Healing a broken bone was easy. Patching up insulted pride wasn't. Sighing, Kelly called the *Sabre*.

Crackling static answered him. He'd forgotten the snoop security. Opening the door, he stepped halfway out into the corridor and called again.

"Standing by for teleport," said Siggerson promptly.

For an instant Kelly indulged himself in the temptation to just beam out and abandon the security officer. But that, of course, was impossible. "Send over Beaulieu with her kit and an extra wristband. We've got an injury."

"What happened?"

Kelly frowned at Caesar, who was now sitting up with 41's support. Prickly independent worlds had pulled out of the

Alliance for less provocation, and Zoe was vital as a buffer zone against the Salukan Empire.

"Kelly?" said Siggerson in alarm. "Are you in trouble over there?"

"Negative," said Kelly, hoping he didn't get hung out to dry over this. "Caesar and 41 have just managed to start a war, that's all. Send over the doctor."

3

The *Sabre* was twice the size of their former ship. When Kelly took his first inspection tour, the spaciousness seemed almost wasteful for a crew of six and one ouoji mascot. But the comfort she offered was undeniably appealing.

Her size permitted a different engine configuration, with a larger light scoop for her photonic drive and enormous XXX reserve batteries from the Ky series for auxiliary power. She had computer-enhanced stabilizers worthy of a battlecruiser. A full round of gravity buffers meant freedom from safety harnesses during entry and exit from time distortion speeds.

As far as speed went, she equalled and even surpassed some of her smaller, proto-class sisters; she could maintain a constant cruising speed of TD 12, with TD 14 available for short emergency bursts.

Her waver shield left almost no ripple and could be operated while underway as well as in orbit. She also came equipped with serious firepower: plasma cannon and long-range torps.

She had three decks. The top deck was comprised of the bridge, light scoop, and armory. The center deck contained the living quarters, mess, recreation lounge, and sickbay. The lower deck had the teleport bay, emergency lifepods, hold, and engines. For all her size, she remained as easy to handle as the *Valiant* had been. In some respects easier, for Siggerson reported that her automateds were more sophisticated. One man could still pilot her.

Kelly sat alone in his quarters, waiting for Caesar and 41 to arrive. He had the lights dimmed to make reading the data viewer easier, but he had long ago finished studying all the data reports available on Kenszana, the Mechtaxlan Cartel which owned it, Cassandra Caliban's bio, the political history of Zoe, and the procedural investigation of the attack upon Caliban's ship. His eyes ached, but not from reading. He glanced at the door of his quarters, wanting to get this over with, yet dreading it.

He had never made such a difficult decision or been so reluctant to give the necessary orders. Maybe he was getting soft. Maybe he was losing the decisive edge necessary for command. He'd never been able to consider a living being expendable. Ships and equipment, yes; men and women, no. That's why he'd left the Fleet and joined Spec. Ops., where lives meant a little more.

A soft chime sounded. He didn't immediately recognize what the sound meant, then the door opened and Caesar peered diffidently inside.

"Come in," said Kelly. His mouth went dry without warning, and his words sounded raspy. He stood up as Caesar and 41 filed inside. Their quick glances around at his quarters betrayed their curiosity.

In the dim light, the muted colors of gold and soft Venetian red took on an extra richness. He had a large study fitted with comfortable chairs, a desk containing a data viewer, comm, and inboard scrambler. Beyond the shadows were a sleeping alcove and the head. His few personal possessions from his temporary leave quarters on Station 4, including his small collection of antique Salukan battle daggers, had been stowed here, but he had yet to arrange anything to make this space his own.

"Sit down, gentlemen," he said.

His discomfiture must have shown, for Caesar stared at him with a frown as he took a seat. 41's gaze was neutral. Both were in crisp uniforms.

"Boss," began Caesar hesitantly, "we're sorry about Nash.

I mean, he deserved what he got, but it makes things harder. I just wanted you to know that we know we deserve the butt chew you're going to give us."

"I apologize to you," said 41. "But to Nash I will not."

Kelly's throat closed off. To hide the fact that he couldn't speak, he resumed his seat behind his desk and scrolled data across his screen. He couldn't read any of it, but it didn't matter.

"No," he said finally. "There isn't time for that. I brought you in here to ask you to volunteer to infiltrate Kenszana."

"Oh," said Caesar blankly.

41 sat forward. "Tell us what to do."

"No, 41," said Kelly gently. This was going to be the hardest for the tall half-breed. "I can't order you to do this. I have to ask you."

41 frowned. "I do not understand."

"Boss, I don't like this," said Caesar uneasily. His green eyes shifted. "What have you cooked up?"

"I see a two-phase approach to Kenszana. As you both know, it's a closed world completely under the control of the Mechtaxlan Cartel. Anyone they don't want in, doesn't get in."

"Yeah, we know that," said Caesar. "We get to play drug smugglers. So?"

Kelly looked at each of them directly. "I want you and 41 to be part of the labor force."

41 shot to his feet. "No!" he said explosively. "Kelly, you go too far."

"41, I know this is difficult—"

41 shook his head. "No, Kelly. I vowed I would never be a slave again. Not for you, not for anyone."

"Hey," said Caesar. "It won't be for real. It's just a disguise. You know, the Slave Hawks—"

"Fool," said 41 with scathing contempt.

Caesar jumped up, fists balled and ready. "Listen, you sorry excuse for a—"

"That's enough!" broke in Kelly sharply. "I told both of you when you came in that this was strictly a volunteer mission."

"Oh, yes, all volunteer," said 41. "Humans are so polite when they want someone to eat filth."

This was much worse than Kelly had expected. He felt his face burning. "You're taking this wrong—"

"I understand you very well. It is a mistake to let a friend become a boss. In time, the friend fades and there is only the boss."

"You don't have to do it."

41's eyes flashed more fiercely than ever. "And if I refuse, what is left? Contempt for my cowardice?"

Caesar whistled. "Why don't you lie on the floor and throw a real tantrum? This isn't any different from any other undercover job we've ever done. Yeah, I know you've been a slave before. Big deal. If you have such a dainty psyche, you shouldn't be in the Hawks at all."

"Caesar, shut up—" began Kelly.

But 41 had already grabbed Caesar by the front of his tunic. In a blur of movement, he shoved the smaller man across the room and slammed him against the wall.

"It is easy, you think?" he said very softly. "There is no pretending to become a slave. There is no putting on a costume and teleporting into the camp. Oh, no, it is not like that. You have to be vended first. And to be sold you have to be prepared. Do you know how to prepare a person for the marketplace, Caesar?"

Caesar's face was twisted in a grimace. "Go to hell."

"Your fingerprints are burned off. You may even be blinded so you can't be identified by a retinal check. Body hair is removed to keep down vermin infestations. You're dipped in disinfectant that leaves your skin raw. If you swallow any of it, it corrodes the lining of your lungs and stomach. Sometimes you are fed a slow-action poison to guarantee that you will die within a year or two. That keeps customers coming back for more labor. You're lined up naked for inspection and sorted according to health and body type for different auctions. Last of all, you're fitted with a slave lock, either on the wrist or the throat."

41 jerked up both sleeves and unfastened the collar of his tunic. His wrists and throat showed white, puckered scars.

"The lock is fused to your skin. Getting it off leaves the scar. If you don't bleed to death in the process, you're left with a reminder the rest of your life that you are a non-identity, a piece of property who belongs to someone out there who paid credits for you. And everyone knows what a slave scar looks like. Its ugliness can be surgically removed. But shame leaves the deepest brand."

Silence fell over the room, broken only by the sounds of harsh breathing. There wasn't going to be violence. Kelly's tense stance relaxed. His palms were damp. Slowly he wiped them dry.

41 drew a deep breath as though to regain control. "Are you ready for that, Caesar?"

Caesar's face was white, but he managed to roll his eyes. "You're overreacting. We won't be going in that way."

"Yes," said Kelly softly, "you will."

Both men's heads jerked in his direction. Kelly walked over to them.

"That's why it has to be your choice. The overseers of rostma harvest and refining are constantly on guard against infiltration. You'll be checked for snoops, implants, false slave locks, the works. You have to be vended on Methanus or you won't be authentic. The least suspicion otherwise, and they'll kill you. If you go in, you'll be strictly on your own."

"Damn," said Caesar. "That's a hard choice, boss. To go with it, how about giving us a talk about our duty and making the galaxy a better place for all? Suicide is always such fun."

"No," said Kelly. "I've looked at alternate plans. If we all go blasting in there together, the Zoans will probably be killed. But if two men are in place in the labor force, searching for the Zoans, the rest of us can go in as smugglers pretending to work a deal. At best, searching will be strictly limited access, but we have a double chance of finding the Zoans."

Caesar snorted. "Limited. You'll be riding high if you get even a peek at the buildings. We'll be knee deep in mud. Lots of searching going on that way. How are you going to get us out?"

Kelly's smile was quick and rueful. "I don't know yet. I was hoping you wouldn't ask me that."

Caesar laughed, but the sound was hollow. "This stinks, boss. 41 is right."

"I know. If both of you refuse, then it's up to me and Nash to go in. I can't use the women for this. They wouldn't be deployed out in the swamp for the root-cutting."

Something cold and narrow entered Caesar's green eyes. "You're going to use Nash?"

"If I have to."

Kelly maintained Caesar's stare until Caesar dropped his gaze.

"Damn, boss," said Caesar. "You put us in a real hole and want us to like it."

"I need your answer," said Kelly. "Yes or no."

Caesar fidgeted, glancing at 41 who stood remote and stone-faced. "Well, I guess I'm in. But I won't work with Nash."

"You won't have to," said Kelly. He rested his hand briefly on Caesar's shoulder. "Thank you."

Then he turned his gaze upon 41. Silence stretched between them. Without a word 41 turned his back on Kelly and strode out.

Kelly let out the breath he'd been holding. He figured he had lost 41's friendship. It hurt.

"I guess that was no," said Caesar.

"Yeah," said Kelly. "I guess it was."

Forty-eight hours later they reached Methanus. It was a misshapen remnant of a planet struck by a comet eons ago. Atmosphere was nominal. The climate consisted of constant winds in the range of thirty to sixty kilometers per hour. Its rotation was irregular, which did weird things to gravity and day length. Spacecraft of all sizes and kinds except military thronged the orbital paths. It was the most prosperous black market in the galaxy.

On Methanus, anything and everything was for sale if you had enough credits. Slaves for labor or household or personal use, trained and untrained. The lovely but almost extinct species of Speimids—gossamer-winged water breathers that could be kept in glass tanks and were prized for the exquisite beauty of their death song. Bulk amounts of contraband and drugs sold cheap enough for high profit margins on regulated worlds. Mercenaries for bodyguards or private armies. Pirated spaceships refitted and given forged registration numbers. Security codes and the latest advances in codebreakers. Classified information from companies or governments.

On the bridge, Kelly stood before the viewscreen which filled one wall, watching the ugly lump of a planet grow larger as Siggerson cut from time distortion speed and brought them in line for orbital approach.

"Anything yet from traffic control?" asked Siggerson.

"Negative," said Phila Mohatsa, their diminuitive electronics expert. She swiveled her chair to glance at Siggerson's master station. "I've told you Methanus doesn't have traffic control."

"That's absurd," said Siggerson. "Sensors are picking up over four hundred vessels on this side alone. There has to be some kind of ordering system to keep them from all running over each other."

"Nope," said Phila cheerfully. She shook her dark curly hair back from her face. "No traffic rules. If you get rammed, tough luck. Methanus is strictly survival of the fittest. I've been here before and—"

She caught Kelly's eye on her and broke off. Red tinged her face, then she looked defiant.

"What were you doing here, toots?" said Caesar, who never missed an opportunity to give Phila a hard time. "Buying nukers or other illegal weapons?"

"As a matter of fact, yes."

They all looked at her, even Siggerson.

Her face got redder. "I wasn't in Special Operations then," she said. "It's none of your business, Caesar."

Kelly said, "You'd better get ready, Caesar. I'll want you in the teleport bay by the time we've established orbit."

Caesar paled. Getting to his feet, he started for the lift without a word. Kelly clasped his hands at his back and began to pace slowly back and forth in front of the viewscreen.

"Incoming long-range transmission from Station 4," said Phila.

Hope flashed through Kelly. Maybe the ambassador had been released and they could all go home. "Hold it, Caesar," said Kelly. "Phila, make sure it's scrambled and share it with Beaulieu down in sickbay."

"Aye, sir."

Phila's small hands danced over her board. Seconds later, Halsey West's face filled the main viewscreen. Old, gruff, and battlescarred, he had run Special Operations since the loss of an arm and leg forced his retirement from the Fleet.

"Hello, Commodore," said Kelly.

"Stand by to receive newest updates on the Caliban situation," said West.

The screen flickered and West's face was replaced by a still shot of Cassandra Caliban. She was dressed in a formal gown that caught the light in hundreds of tiny starbursts. Her auburn hair had been knotted at the base of her neck, and Zoan blue diamonds dangled from her ears. The sight of her never failed to make something twinge in the pit of Kelly's stomach.

West's voice said, "The Mechtaxlan Cartel is still denying any direct involvement in the kidnapping. But a spokesman claiming to belong to a legalize-all-drugs coalition has made ransom demands. Intelligence has traced sponsorship of this coalition to Mechtaxlan.

"The spokesman also claims that Cassandra Caliban is being held on an unmarked asteroid in Quadrant 2. Unless the Zoan transponders have been removed and transferred to Kenszana as a diversion—and the Zoan government insists that the transponders will not work if removed—we have no reason to alter our perception of where she is being held."

"What about the ransom demands?" asked Kelly. "Will they be met?"

West frowned. "Despite pressure from Zoan officials, the Alliance Council has deemed the terms unacceptable. They will not be met. What is your progress, Commander?"

Kelly made sure his disappointment did not show. "We are implementing phase one of our recovery plan."

"Very well. Intelligence agents are impersonating Zoan officials in an effort to spin out ransom negotiations for as long as possible."

"Good," said Kelly. "A flat no at this point would probably get the ambassador killed."

"Negotiations cannot be strung out forever. You don't have much time to put your operatives in place."

"We'll have enough," said Kelly. Now was not the time to mention that one of his operatives had mutinied.

"Zoe is highly reluctant to leave this matter in our hands. It's been difficult to keep the Zoan armada from striking out for Kenszana. If you fail to recover the ambassador, Zoe will probably secede from the Alliance. It may even declare war."

Kelly swallowed hard. "I understand, sir."

"Swift flight, Kelly. West out."

The screen blanked.

"That was nothing," said Phila indignantly. "Lots of talk and no results. Typical bureaucratic procedure. It's obvious Mechtaxlan is blowing smoke. I say we ought to bomb them out."

"Yeah," said Caesar eagerly. "I could smuggle in some nice little molded explosives—"

"Taking out the installation is not our job," said Kelly. "We're strictly rescue this time."

Caesar sighed and shook his head. "Losing your flair, boss. Once upon a time, we would have done both."

Kelly glared at him. "You're supposed to be getting ready, Samms."

"So I'm going. Yusus, what a grouch," muttered Caesar.

"Hey, Caesar," called Phila just before he got on the lift.

Caesar paused and glanced back.

She gave him a thumbs up. "Swift flight and home again."

"Yes," said Siggerson. "Good luck."

Caesar made an effort to smile. "Thanks."

The lift swallowed him. Kelly frowned and kept his gaze on the viewscreen. He intended to go with Caesar as the second man, but he worried that in his absence Nash would try to take command. 41 could prevent that if he would. Kelly could even place 41 in temporary command. But 41 at best was no leader of people; at worst he was completely unpredictable. Right now he was at his worst. As for taking Nash undercover, from what Kelly could determine Nash had no undercover experience. Now was not the time for a training mission with a hot-headed colonist.

"Phila," said Kelly, "send that coded message to our contact down on the planet."

"Yes, sir."

"Kelly," said Siggerson, "that traffic pattern is madness. I've been tracking it, and there's a ship playing chicken with the others. Two near collisions in the last eight minutes."

"The pilot must be lifting," said Phila. "Maybe snorting. Maybe even in-lining. It's very fashionable for civilian pilots to do togi. Heightens their reflexes."

"Nonsense," said Siggerson with all the disdain of a professional pilot for the amateur. "It slices depth perception and causes a false sense of competence. I'm not taking a new ship into that. We'll lock into a geosynchronous path at forty thousand kilometers, which is just within teleport range. But if necessary we can stay out of that madman's path."

Kelly's brows shot up. "Forty is within range? Since when?"

Siggerson's gaunt face broke into a grin. "More engine power means longer range."

Kelly nodded, feeling like an idiot. "Of course."

"Commander," said Phila.

Kelly went to her station where a small viewscreen came to life. The transmission was all broken up, showing only garish bands of color, wave shifts, and the vague shadow of a head beyond.

"Contact is using heavy scrambler," said Phila apologetically. "I've tried combing the signal to clean up our reception, but it's no go."

"Safer for him if we accept it this way," said Kelly. "Open audio."

Static crackled over the speakers. ". . . in luck," said a voice that swelled and unraveled from octave to octave as transmission speeds varied. "Private sale arranged to fill two gaps in quota sale to Mechtaxlan. Ship leaving in two hours. Supply . . . get them aboard."

"Good work," said Kelly, aware that two slaves had been abducted and possibly resold or killed to create that gap. But his orders from West were clear: achieve rescue of the Zoans at any cost. "What are the teleport coordinates?"

The signal shattered to an abrupt end. Phila had a small receiver in her ear. She frowned and began keying her translator board with rapid strokes.

"Got it," she said seconds later. "The computer will decode and route the coordinates directly to the teleport bay. Everything's set."

"Good. Be sure and—"

"Kelly," said Siggerson. "A silent alarm just went off in the armory. It's been unlocked and entered."

Kelly whirled. "What?"

"Probably Nash," said Phila. "We shouldn't have sent that report down to sickbay. Beaulieu says he's suffering from a guilt complex as big as a—"

"I'll take care of it," said Kelly.

He left the bridge fast, his stride long and angry. The armory door was open, but the lock mechanism looked intact. Kelly went inside. He would worry later about how the lock code had been broken.

But it wasn't Nash. 41, whom Kelly hadn't seen since he had refused to take the mission, stood at the handweapons rack. He was sighting a laser-scoped Sony Wesson .47 with a single muzzle and heat-seeking bullets with splinter jackets. It was new and nasty, but then 41 wasn't a particularly merciful killer.

He was out of uniform and instead wore a sleeveless jerkin, tight leather trousers, and soft boots of lyx hide. A knife and scabbard were strapped to his upper left arm. Another scabbard holding illegal laser wings was strapped to the inside of his forearm.

Surprised, Kelly experienced a sharp rush of hope that 41 had changed his mind. But the hostility in those yellow eyes made him think twice.

"Hello, 41," he said softly. "Jumping ship?"

41 grunted. He tucked a spare ammo clip into his pocket along with a soft gel bomb and a couple of field ration packets.

"I suppose those weapons can constitute your severance pay," said Kelly angrily. "But you won't leave without installation of mind blocks."

41 glanced at him. "You think I would sell Hawk information?"

"It's a living."

41 shrugged. "As you say."

"Dammit, 41!"

"What do you want from me, Kelly?" retorted 41. "I have changed myself much to conform to your life, to the life of a Hawk. I have done your will without complaint. But I do not kill myself for you. Slavery is death. You do not understand."

"Yes, I do."

41 tapped his temple. "Up here, perhaps." He poked Kelly hard in the chest. "Here, no."

"41—"

"I saw your life, your Earth, your family. I saw your ways. Soft ways. All the instincts of a Hawk have been learned, put on like clothes. But in the jungle of live or die, there are no clothes. What you know means nothing. It is what you are and how you react which keeps you alive." He shook his head. "Why did you ask me to go back into that?"

Kelly swallowed, forcing down anger, trying to remain clear-headed. "Because you're the strongest of the squad. You know what is—"

41 snorted. "You send Caesar into death and want me to protect him. That is why you asked me."

"41—"

"Now you are a greater fool. You will go in my place. You know less than Caesar. Why do you blind yourself, Kelly?"

"I have a job to do," said Kelly through his teeth. "I joined the Hawks because I have abilities most civilians lack. I can help people in trouble by using those abilities. Just because the job gets unpleasant at times doesn't mean I'm free to drop it. That isn't what responsibility and commitment are about."

"Words," said 41 scornfully. "Many words. No sense. Goodbye, Kelly."

He stalked out. Furious, Kelly went after him.

"Wait a minute!" he called after 41. "You're reporting to sickbay. While I'm getting my transponder implant, Beaulieu can start implementing those security blocks."

"You won't keep your implants. They'll be taken out."

Kelly thought about his contact waiting on Methanus to slip him into the slave consignment. "Maybe. Maybe not."

41 bared his teeth in scorn and kept walking. Kelly matched his stride. Together they got into the lift.

"Deck two," said Kelly.

The lift started down.

41 frowned. "It is good to go. This ship creates more softness. Lifts instead of ladders. Not even a button to push. Instead you speak and the command is done."

"You could be on an Othian ship where the computers are organic and half of the commands are given telepathically," said Kelly.

41 made no reply. The lift doors opened and they stepped off. They encountered Ouoji in the corridor leading to sickbay. She had been avoiding the bridge lately, which was unusual because she preferred to sit on the corner of Siggerson's master board.

Kelly wondered if she knew 41 was leaving yet. "Hello, Ouoji," he said.

She flicked the tip of her silky tail in greeting, but did not slow her brisk pace. Her usually immaculate fur looked rumpled.

"Going somewhere?" called Kelly after her.

Her tail flicked again but she kept walking. *She knows 41 is leaving*, he thought.

"See?" said 41. "This ship is too comfortable. It makes everyone lose edge. Even Ouoji is getting fat."

That got a reaction. Ouoji stopped and glanced over her shoulder with a distinct glare in her blue eyes. She flared her ear flaps, then clamped them tightly to her skull and trotted away.

"Very tactful," said Kelly, trying not to smile. "Now you've insulted her."

"I meant to," said 41. "She has been stealing food from the galley."

"Ouoji wouldn't do that!"

41 shrugged.

Kelly frowned. A disgruntled mascot was one more problem he didn't need. "It must be stress. Maybe she doesn't like the new ship."

"It is probably because she can't use the lift," said 41. "How can she tell it where to take her?"

Kelly paused just short of the sickbay doors and looked straight at 41. "I don't want you to go."

41's yellow eyes met his. They were as impersonal as glass. He said nothing at all.

The sickbay doors opened. Beaulieu stood there with her arms crossed over her lab smock. "Caesar's already come and gone," she said. "What are the two of you waiting for? A printed invitation?"

Tall and rangy, with skin the color of light chocolate and short-cropped hair sprinkled with gray, the doctor had an astringent manner and a warm heart. Her dark eyes scanned them. "41's in costume. I guess he's the one who loses his implants?"

"Wrong," said Kelly. "I lose the implants. 41 wants mind blocks."

He had thought his voice was perfectly even and controlled. But Beaulieu's eyes narrowed. She shot a glance at each of them again. Stepping into the corridor, she let the door close behind her.

"I thought you two had patched up your quarrel by now. What's going on?"

"Is Nash in there?"

"Yes. Undergoing his last session under the regenerative lamp for his leg. He can't hear unless you start shouting. When are you going to answer my question?"

"41 is jumping ship," said Kelly. It came out harsher than he intended.

41 had on his stone face. He said nothing.

"He can't leave the service without being blocked," said Kelly. "He knows too much classified information."

Beaulieu's brows crawled up. "Official desensitization requires a full . . . Kelly, I don't have the equipment here to do everything properly."

"Finesse isn't necessary," snapped Kelly.

She knew when to back off. She did so now. "All right," she said, throwing up her hands. "But it will take time."

"My implants first," said Kelly. "I've got to get down to the surface as soon as possible."

"If you're going with Caesar, who's going to mind the store?"

"Siggerson."

Beaulieu snorted. "I'd like to see him lead a mission."

"He won't go down to Kenszana," said Kelly. "You and Phila will—"

"—be stuck with Nash," said Beaulieu angrily. "No way, Kelly! That man is a classic paranoid. As soon as this treatment is finished and he can walk again, he's going to be all over this ship. He's—"

"Nash has no authority over any of you," said Kelly with equal sharpness. "Remember that. Siggerson is in command. But you and Phila will have to take care of the second phase. We've been over it enough. I know you can handle it."

She glared at 41, and although she said nothing, the meaning of her look was plain. It was a hell of a time for him to leave.

"Let's get on with it," said Kelly.

Beaulieu clamped her lips together tightly. She touched the door latch and it slid open.

"After you, gentlemen," she said.

4

Antoinette Beaulieu was a woman who did not put up with
nonsense. As soon as Kelly had changed from his uniform to
a costume of rags, collected Caesar, and teleported down to
Methanus, she turned on 41.

"It's time for some answers—"

Her voice died off as she saw the pistol aimed at her
midsection. It looked capable of splattering her across the
sickbay with one shot. She dragged her gaze up from it and met
41's amber eyes. They had a sheen of hostility and determination. There was no awareness of her as a colleague; he stared
at her as he would any obstacle. In that instant, she believed he
would shoot her.

Fear trickled through her, but she refused to let it take over.
Her first priority was to show that she was not afraid of him.
Then she could talk him out of this.

She said, "You aren't going to shoot me with that, so put it
away. I want to know why—"

"You will not mess with my mind," said 41. Keeping the
gun trained on her, he started backing toward the door.

"I don't intend to," she snapped. "I never did. Whatever is

45

going on between you and Kelly? What's all this about a resignation?"

41 bared his teeth; it was not a smile. "Kelly calls it mutiny."

"Unless you incite the whole squad to abandon the mission with you, it's hardly mutiny. Desertion, maybe, only I can't believe you would just run away. Will you put that gun down? I keep no weapons in sickbay. I couldn't overpower you if I tried."

"You have other tricks," 41 said, but he lowered the gun.

Relief flooded her. She wanted to close her eyes and sag into the nearest chair. Instead she kept her voice crisp. "Thank you. Now please tell me what is going on. What are you up to?"

"There is no mystery," he said. "I am leaving. Kelly has become a fool."

She frowned at his evasiveness. "For once in your life, would you try to remember that I am not your enemy? No one on board this ship is. We're your people, 41. We stick together. We help each other. We've all risked death together more times than I want to count. Tell me what's wrong. Let me help."

"You don't want to help," said 41. "You want me to stay because I am needed for the mission. You are afraid of carrying out phase two without Kelly as leader. You want me to take the responsibility for you. I will not."

He turned to go.

"41!"

He glanced back.

Beaulieu stepped forward. She hoped her expression was still showing concern, because inside she was a mess of seething frustration. What good was all of her psychology training? She should have more insight on this operative by now. But she felt as though she were trying to stare through a wall of opaque glass.

Her instincts said to trust 41. He had never let them down yet. But her mind was remembering that psych report in his file conducted at his induction into the Hawks. A report which listed strong instabilities at key personality points and urged his rejection by the service. Kelly had ignored that report and convinced West to ignore it also.

But if 41 had turned, her duty lay in following Kelly's last orders.

"41," she said more gently, trying to reach him another way. "I'm aware that Kelly asked you to go undercover as a slave. It upset you, didn't it? Kelly was afraid it would. He hoped you would understand why he asked that of you. Not to degrade you, but to indicate his trust in your strength and abilities—"

41 moved quicker than she believed possible. One moment he was by the door, the next he had gripped her tunic and was shoving her backward into a console of biopsy scanners. His eyes had narrowed to slits; his mouth was clamped tight. Fury traveled into her from him like bolts of energy, raw and hurtful. She realized he was projecting his emotions into her, using them to hurt her as he never had before. This must be why he didn't like to be touched. The empathic threshold must be difficult to block.

But there was no time to analyze the situation. He was hurting her physically as well, pressing her lower back against the corner of the console so that it gouged deeply into her right kidney. She gasped with pain, and hated him for rendering her helpless so easily.

Giving him a sharp kick, which he blocked with a shift of his leg, she glared at him. "Get your damned hands off of me, 41! Let me go—"

"I am not a pet," he said, his voice clipped with anger. "I am not stupid."

"No one said you were."

"You patronize me, Doctor. You think if you make enough soothing noises I will quieten and become willing again to follow at Kelly's heels like a dog." 41 moved his face closer to hers, close enough for her to see the fine texture of his bronzed skin, close enough for her to feel the heat of his breath. "Never do that again."

She froze, instinct warning her not to provoke him further. When she neither moved nor spoke, he released her. The abrupt cessation of pressure on her back made her gasp aloud with relief. She bent forward, fighting off the urge to throw the chair at him.

41 headed for the door.

She forced herself to straighten. "If you leave this ship without implementation of the mind blocks, you will be in violation of—"

41 snarled something rude.

"Dammit, 41! Listen to me! You'll be arrested and charged with conspiracy to impart classified—"

41 slammed his hand on the latch and the door slid open. He glared at her over his shoulder. "Leave me alone! I do not care about your laws and your regulations. I do not care about any of you!"

"That's enough," said Nash, appearing from the adjoining treatment room.

Startled, Beaulieu gestured at him to stay put. She didn't need his interference. But the colonel ignored her. His gaze was locked on 41.

"You will be treated as ordered by your commanding officer. You will submit at this time. You will not leave this area until you have done so."

41's mouth twisted into a mocking smile. "You will go to hell," he said and fired his pistol.

Beaulieu screamed. The recoil and the sound of shattering glass were simultaneous. The readout panel scant centimeters to the left of Nash's head exploded, driving Nash and Beaulieu to the floor as sparks showered everywhere. Wiring caught fire, and panels around the lab area shorted in swift succession.

Ducking sparks, Beaulieu forced herself to her feet. "41!" she shouted.

But he was gone.

She kicked the chair out of her way. "Damn!"

"That creature is insane," said Nash, still on his knees beneath a rain of sparks. "I intend to file a charge of attempted murder—"

Beaulieu snorted, shoving past him to hit the fire containment switch. A fine dust of chemicals rained from the ceiling, making her sneeze and cough.

She bent over and grasped Nash's sleeve. "Come on. Out of here. It's a bad idea to breathe this stuff."

Nash staggered to his feet and limped after her into the corridor.

She switched on the nearest wall comm. "Beaulieu speaking. Shut down the teleport bay. Fast."

"Doctor?" said Siggerson's voice. "What's going on in sickbay? Internal sensors are registering an electrical fire."

"It's under control, Siggerson. Just shut down the teleport, will you? 41 is trying to leave the ship—"

"He's already gone," said Siggerson. "Shall I call him on his wrist comm?"

She leaned her forehead upon the cold surface of the wall. "No," she said, sighing. "Kelly is going to have our hides."

"What was that?"

Nash shouldered her aside. "This is Colonel Nash speaking. I want Operative 41 reported to the authorities for attempted murder and—"

"He didn't try to murder you," snapped Beaulieu. "You had no business interfering at all."

Nash glared at her. "I see. Sticking together, no matter how much evidence points the other way. I shall file full charges at the first opportunity, and if I am not given cooperation I'll name every crewmember of this ship as accomplices."

"Don't be a bigger idiot than you already are," said Beaulieu, long past tactfulness. "41 doesn't miss. If he'd wanted to kill you, he would have."

The lift at the end of the corridor opened before Nash could sputter a retort, and Mohatsa came running.

"Beaulieu! Siggerson sent me down here to check out what's happening. You okay?"

Beaulieu nodded, glad to see her. "Yes. We're waiting for the dust to smother the fire."

"What's all this about 41 leaving the ship? I thought he was supposed to stay—"

"No," Beaulieu said grimly. "He's jumped. Kelly gave orders for me to put security mind blocks on him, but 41 refused to let me do it."

"And he tried to kill me," said Nash. "I'm filing charges against all of you for incompetence and insubordination."

Phila's black eyes swept over him. "Who asked you?"

His face turned scarlet. "If your rudeness is typical of the whole Alliance, we Zoans want no part of it! I want long-range communications immediately to contact my—"

"No," said Phila.

His eyes widened. "No? How dare you—"

Phila slipped her prong from her sleeve and snapped out one blade. She held it up. "Let me explain this once, Colonel. We are in mission. That means no unnecessary personal calls breaking our security net."

"You have no authority to deny me contact with my government!"

Phila glanced at Beaulieu. "Can't you fit him with a tranquilizer patch and get him out of our hair? We're supposed to break orbit in seven minutes."

Nash growled something unmentionable and strode away.

Beaulieu blew out a loud breath. "That's one idiot I could do without. He actually tried to give 41 orders."

Phila shrugged. "He carries no weight around here. If he gets to be too much of a problem, we'll confine him to quarters. Now, will you tell me about 41? Are we supposed to get him back, or what?"

"I'd like to see one of us try," said Beaulieu sarcastically.

"Yeah, you're right. He's one big, *scatsi* devil when he wants to be." Phila shoved her hair out of her face. "Hokay, that's the end of him. Kelly had already scrubbed him off the mission. We proceed as ordered for phase two. I figure the ambassador is more important."

Beaulieu agreed. "If she's anything like Nash, she deserves what's happened to her."

"You got that. Why don't we put sleepy gas in his air system?"

Beaulieu looked at her sharply. "Are you serious?"

"Yeah."

"I'll do it."

Phila laughed and gave her a slap on the arm. "You're okay, Doc. I'm going back to the bridge. We've got work to do."

"What about 41?"

The amusement faded from Phila's face. "I'm not reporting him," she said. "That's the commander's job."

Beaulieu frowned. She hated the typical operative attitude of shoving all responsibility onto officers. But she didn't want to report 41 either.

"We'll be giving him a hell of a head start," she said slowly. "Internal Affairs will be after us for this."

"You really think he's turned?"

"I don't know. It's always unwise to let emotions and sentiment color facts." Beaulieu met Phila's eyes. "We need him, you know. Kelly's put Siggerson in command, but Siggerson has to stay with the ship. That leaves me and you for phase two." She paused a moment. "And Nash."

"Hah! No way he is going with us."

"Fine. You and me." Beaulieu couldn't make herself admit her feelings of inadequacy for this. She was no leader.

Phila didn't look worried. "We'll handle our part, Doc. We make a good team. You want help cleaning up the sickbay?"

"No thanks. I can handle it."

"Right. Give me an estimate on wiring damage as soon as you can."

"There's a lot," said Beaulieu drily.

"More specific than that, please."

Phila headed down the corridor, leaving Beaulieu standing there wishing for thirty less years and a lot more confidence. The ambassador's chances were looking poorer all the time.

Teleporting to Methanus was like beaming straight into hell. From the first moment Kelly couldn't draw a full breath of air. The multiple oxygen compound Beaulieu had given them must be doing its job because they weren't asphyxiating, but his lungs kept jerking in a panic. A gale-force wind nearly buffeted him off his feet as soon as he materialized. Kelly and Caesar hung onto each other to keep upright. Minute grains of sand whipped up by the wind stung like bullets.

"Damn, boss! I can't see a thing," said Caesar.

Kelly shielded his face with a raised hand, squinting in an effort to take his bearings. As near as he could tell, they were in some sort of back alley. The buildings were of different heights and styles, all looking cheaply constructed. Most shimmered behind force walls.

Staggering along the alley, which served as a wind tunnel, Kelly bumped from side to side, trying to protect his face, feeling as though the wind was whipping away what little air reached his nostrils. His clothes billowed and shredded.

The street ahead of them flashed with light and color. Gigantic holo ads competed in garishness for attention on both ground and air levels. One such ad was of a woman who stood straddling the street, her short skirt billowing. Pedestrians walking beneath her looked straight up at a flashing club name and street address.

Caesar gawked, the street signs flashing sickly yellows and greens across his face. "Hey, I could get used to this. Maybe we'll have time to stop by—"

"Come on," said Kelly.

The crowds on the streets were plentiful but not thick. No one jostled or bumped into anyone else if they could avoid it. Two men—one a Jostic whose fashionable, wired hair looked odd with his bowed legs, crooked back, and furrowed brow plate, and the other a Minzanese in goggles and atmosphere mask—stopped in the crosswalk and ended their argument with a shootout. The Jostic died screaming. Stepping over him, the Minzanese brushed a hand across his crackling body armor to reset it, and left his victim in the path of the ground traffic surging forward.

Overhead, sleek aircars shimmering behind shields paused to hover, either watching the street action or conducting deals in the safety of the air. Hungry-eyed punks roamed, searching for easy marks or frantically signalling to be approached. Naked males and females of varied species gyrated in cages suspended on grav-flats outside clubs. Terrified children crouched in shielded display bubbles, flinching from the avid faces staring at them. Winged creatures that were all light and air, as transparent as glass yet shimmering with phosphorescence, floated through the holos and dived occasionally toward the pedestrians. Their huge jewel-like eyes enticed, causing music to burst within their victims' minds, and they drew the unwary away into the darkness.

Mercenaries lounged in doorways, weapons cradled casually in their arms, their eyes bored and indifferent. Others sat at tables in the street cafes, their clothes worn, their bodies hard, putting themselves up for sale. They made Kelly think of 41. He caught himself looking too closely at faces, hoping. It was foolish. He stopped looking.

"Just one bar, boss," Caesar pleaded, gazing longingly at doorways standing open behind force walls. Music, drug-laden smoke, and voice babble rolled out from these places. "I'm working up a powerful thirst."

"We don't have time," said Kelly. "One more block and we'll be at the market."

Caesar frowned. "Even condemned men get a last drink."

"Don't be morbid," said Kelly. "We're hardly condemned."

A man emerged from the crowd ahead of them and deliberately blocked their path. He was dressed in a tent-shaped tunic ending just above his knees, with wide sleeves and a cowled neck. The wind shifted the garb about his thin body. From the tunic's stiffness, Kelly suspected it was heavily armored.

Kelly put his arm across Caesar to hold him back. "Careful."

"Yusus! We're not going to tiptoe around every boo-head we come across, are we?"

Kelly glared at Caesar, wondering how he could be thickheaded enough to forget they had no weapons. "This is no time to pick a fight," he said.

"Huh? Oh." Caesar's belligerence faded. "Uh, yeah. Right. No trouble."

Kelly stepped around the man. But the stranger moved again to stand in the way. Tension tightened low in Kelly's gut. From the corner of his left eye he saw a group of people, richly dressed and of three sexes, watching with obvious enjoyment. They were cracking jokes and laying bets, but Kelly couldn't understand a word of what they were saying. He missed his translator acutely. Until now he hadn't realized how much he depended on it.

But maybe it was just as well he couldn't understand their insults.

"Look," he said, lifting his hands to the stranger. "No trouble. I want no trouble with you. Let me pass."

A scream pierced the air. Startled, Kelly glanced up and saw a drug-wasted punk being lifted into the air by one of the winged hunters. The boy twisted and struggled in the creature's arms, screaming for help, but there was none.

The stranger glanced up also. Hoping for this, Kelly seized his chance and darted around the man. He broke into a run, with Caesar following close on his heels. The wind was in their faces; trying to run against it was like trying to plow through a force wall. When little black dots started dancing before his vision, Kelly slowed down. He struggled to breathe. Behind him he could hear Caesar wheezing.

Kelly glanced back. He didn't see the stranger. "So much for that," he said in relief.

The stranger winked into existence in front of them, blocking their path once again.

Kelly skidded to a halt. Caesar bumped into him from behind.

"What the hell—"

Kelly grabbed Caesar's arm in growing alarm. "Belt tele-port," he said.

"But that's impossible. Just a theoretical—"

Kelly shoved Caesar to the left, pushing him into an alley. It was lit by one dim halogen street lamp that turned everything a queer shade of orange. They stumbled over a ragged creature huddled in a doorway, and plowed through knee-high piles of trash blown into the alley by the wind. Ahead of them a winged hunter swooped down from the shadows, orange light filtering through its transparent wings.

"Watch out!" said Kelly. He glanced over his shoulder, searching for an unlocked doorway, an unshielded cellar window, anywhere to hide.

"What the hell are these things?" asked Caesar, coughing and wheezing. He pressed his chest as though it hurt. "I can't breathe."

Kelly was too busy gulping in air to answer. The hunter floated down to eye level, its glowing wings outstretched almost to the walls on either side of the alley. Behind them came the stranger, walking ever closer. If he had been their contact, he would have indicated it by now. Since he hadn't, Kelly had to assume he was an enemy, possibly some press gang enforcer. Methanus was no place to visit unarmed. Kelly began to wish he had listened to 41.

"Hey, it's kind of pretty," said Caesar. "Kind of like a big butterfly. I saw some in a museum once. But these are free."

Frowning, Kelly glanced at him. "Caesar?"

But Caesar was staring at the creature as though mesmer-ized. Ignoring Kelly, he stepped toward it.

Kelly grabbed his arm. "No, Caesar! Don't look at it!"

The creature's eyes flashed at Kelly, and his mind exploded with vivid colors. He staggered to one side, putting his hands to his head. Dimly he was aware of the danger. He must resist, but the colors kaleidoscoped through his mind, drenching him. And as they blended and melted into ever-changing hues, he heard music, weird-scaled and alien, yet inescapable. He clapped his hands over his ears, but the music was in his mind. It drew him forward in spite of his efforts to remain where he was.

Caesar was already ahead of him, moving eagerly to the outstretched arms of the hunter. From overhead Kelly glimpsed a second one coming, wings rippling in the wind as the creature angled for a graceful descent into the narrow alley. Fear ran through Kelly, and for an instant the music faded in his mind. He stopped, gasping and trying to pull away.

"Caesar!" he called.

But even as he spoke the music swelled over him, engulfing his senses. Crying out, he sank to his knees. The second hunter hovered above him, its wings glowing in the shadows, its limbs reaching out to him.

Talons as clear as glass hooked into Kelly's shoulders. Pain like white heat went through him. He screamed.

A blue-white bolt of plasma slammed into the hunter. It shrilled its agony straight across the telepathic link into Kelly. He screamed with it. The outstretched wings crumpled, and it fell, driving Kelly beneath it to the ground. He lay there, stunned beneath its weight. The stench of burned flesh and blood filled the air.

With a screech, the other hunter rose with a furious beating of its wings. A second plasma bolt missed it by centimeters. It continued to rise into the air until it was out of range, and then flew off, still screaming in rage.

The colors and music vanished from Kelly's mind. He pressed his cheek against the gritty pavement in relief, closing his eyes to savor the welcome black silence inside his head.

A hand clutched his shoulder, bringing a muffled cry of pain from him, "Don't, Caesar," he said. "Leave me here."

But it wasn't Caesar who was dragging him out from under the dead creature. The man in the tent-shaped tunic grunted with the effort of shifting him. When Kelly was clear, the stranger pulled him to a sitting position. Kelly winced, touching his shoulder and feeling sticky blood.

"Idiot," muttered the man in a heavily accented version of street Glish. "Lower prices when you're marked."

"Hey," said Caesar. "Get away from him, boo-head!"

Still kneeling, the stranger turned to aim his weapon at Caesar.

Hastily Caesar lifted his hands. "Take it easy with that thing."

The stranger muttered something and glanced along the alley as though fearing interference would come by at any moment.

"Well," said Kelly, squinting as the world began to tilt around him. He shivered. "Thanks for the help."

"No help if you die of kyriax poisoning," said the stranger, pulling out a couple of patches from his pocket. Ripping bigger tears in Kelly's shabby tunic, he slapped a patch across the deepest part of each wound, where full potency could enter Kelly's bloodstream in the least amount of time.

Whatever drug the patches contained, it worked fast. Almost at once the pain faded. Kelly let out his breath in relief. His depth perception was distorted, warping objects around him, and his own heartbeat pounded against his eardrums, but at least the world no longer threatened to go woozy and dark on him.

He blinked at the stranger, finding clear focusing difficult. "Thanks again."

"What is that stuff?" asked Caesar suspiciously. "What are you giving him?"

"Tapo," said the stranger.

"The hell you are!" said Caesar. "That stuff's addictive. Get away from him."

The stranger's eyes were as flat and as lacking in expression as an android's. He kept his weapon trained on Caesar, his thumb flat upon the firing button.

"We'll put him through a public sonic shower on the way to get rid of the bloodstains. After that, he'll pass as just another junk-head. His market price won't be as low that way. If we are favored, the goods inspector won't catch the wounds. Help me lift him on his feet."

"No," said Caesar. "You may be some street cleaner out to meet your quota, but you can do it without us."

Caesar lifted his arm to activate his wristband.

Kelly tipped back his head. "No, Caesar," he said, feeling the strangest urge to laugh. Life was pretty good. Even the dead hunter smelled good. He grinned broadly, floating. "Meet our contact. Right, stranger? Contact. Taking us off to work. Yeah."

Caesar's head kept expanding and contracting. Kelly worried about him. That must hurt.

"You okay, Samms?" he asked worriedly.

"I'm fine," said Caesar. He put his hand on Kelly's head and pressed Kelly's face against his leg. "Take it easy, boss. Float where it takes you. Keep it a good trip."

"Hot down here," said Kelly.

"Yeah, I'll bet." Caesar glared at the stranger. Right now only that slagger in his hand kept Caesar from breaking his jaw and most of the other bones in his body. Not that the boo-head would care. From the glassy stare of his eyes, the lack of expression, and a certain rhythm of his head shifts, Caesar had already decided he was running on full bio-ware, wired and jacked in to some air circuit frequency that told him what to say and do. He smelled faintly of chemicals, which meant he was on drugs like amniozine and teletrine to keep his body from rejecting the wire implants in his brain. And he probably ran on tapo to keep himself from losing tolerance for the other drugs. A real prize of humanity.

"Okay," said Caesar very quietly. "If you're our contact, prove it."

The stranger turned his left palm upright. A silver glow from the diodes inset there winked in the Alliance code pattern.

Caesar tried to suck in a rapid breath, found himself choking, and forced his lungs to calm down. Slow, shallow breaths. But his brain felt fuzzy from the lack of enough oxygen. He yawned and frowned.

"Why didn't you show us that at the first and save us this little party?"

The stranger blinked once, as slowly as a reptile. He gave Caesar the creeps.

"IDs aren't flashed on the streets," the stranger said. "Help me stand him up. We don't have much time to vend you. This late, maybe we can avoid the dip vat and having your fingerprints sliced off."

A chill ran through Caesar. He put a protective arm around Kelly. "Kelly's going back to the ship. He needs medical attention."

"He'll get it once he's vended. There isn't much time if you want on that Kenszana shipment." The stranger hesitated, then added, "Also, I don't have much more free time before I go back on frequency."

Caesar stared at him with revulsion. "You really work on wire?"

"Isn't it obvious? Stand him up."

Kelly chuckled, making Caesar look down at him. Kelly's blue eyes, ordinarily razor keen, were glazed behind a thin white film. Little nerve twitches kept running through his face. His mouth was slack. In just minutes, Caesar's sharp-witted commander had turned into a junk-head. Caesar was worried sick about him. He didn't know much about tapo, except it was one of the bad ones. Not as bad as rostma, but bad enough. Kelly was doing okay right now, but when he began to come down . . . all Caesar needed was for the boss to start tweaking.

"Gotta work," muttered Kelly.

Caesar shook his head and activated his wrist comm. The stranger put the muzzle of his slagger right in Caesar's face, close enough for Caesar to smell the heat still lingering inside the bore.

"No," said the stranger. "Your comm transmission will trigger my code activation. Once I go on frequency I can't help you. This is your only chance to be on that shipment. Do you want it or not?"

"No," said Caesar.

"Yes," said Kelly.

Caesar frowned, looking for the man he had followed loyally for nearly seven years behind the glazed eyes and twitching. "Boss, you sure about this?"

Kelly's fingers fumbled to grip his hand; they dug in. "F-finish job," he said and went off into a bout of giggling. "Happy work. All day long."

Caesar winced. "Damn," he whispered. "I guess we're still in. Come on, boss, up on your feet."

5

Harva Opie lived on Methanus, somewhere. If he was still alive. Rumor said he now owned the best mercenary army in the galaxy. If true, Harva Opie had come a long way from leading a motley band of soldiers for hire.

41 slitted his eyes against the howling wind. He walked with his head tucked low and dragged in breaths from the side, the way a swimmer does. The harsh industrial stinks upon the air made it difficult to trace scents. The wind made it hard to hear or see. He walked fast with his pistol drawn and ready in his hand. No one bumped into him or tried to panhandle him. He knew which signals not to make.

His anger only fueled his alertness. His senses were hair-trigger ready. He wanted to kill something.

It should not matter so much, being out of the Hawks. He had never belonged anywhere, would never belong. He would never be human either, no matter how much he tried.

Now he had stopped trying.

Club lights flashed, using bright colors and subliminal messages to draw in customers. 41 scanned the signs, looking for the symbol of a notched circle. When he found a club bearing that sign of ownership, he entered.

The porter let him through the force wall after a demand that he holster his weapon. 41 complied. He did not have to worry about any requests to leave his weapons at the door. This establishment was not for soft people.

The club was below street level. Descending the steps, 41 saw Jostics—hulking and deformed, speaking to each other with swift, gutteral laughter, and dressed in rich materials in need of cleaning—mercenaries of all species, even a pair of Salukans in hooded cloaks whispering in a corner. 41 waded through a fog of blue smoke, drugged incense, and flickering table holos in traditional and alien pornographic styles. The latter made him remember Caesar's Hobari dancer and Kelly's embarrassment over it. Kelly could have ordered Caesar to get rid of it, but he hadn't. 41 frowned. Now was not a time to think of Kelly's kindness. Kelly was too soft; soon he would be dead.

The stench of spilled liquor permeated every other odor. The waiters were alive, rather than droids, which meant the prices were high. 41 hadn't come to drink, however. He made his way straight to the bar, ignoring a waiter's attempts to seat him at a table where he would be automatically charged for a minimum of two drinks.

On the tiny stage, decorated by two speimid tanks containing half-dead occupants, a band played lojan jazz at a hot, sweaty tempo. No one was listening. No one was dancing.

The bartender flicked 41 a bored glance. "This isn't a stand-up bar. Take a table or clear out."

"I want Harva," said 41.

"Don't know—"

41 reached over the bar and gripped the man by the throat. A proteetive cartilage band beneath the skin told 41 that he was Salukan, surgically altered to look human, but still Salukan. 41 didn't care. His fingers were strong enough to crack through that cartilage, and he used enough pressure to let the bartender know it.

"I want Harva," he said. "This club belongs to him."

"He ain't here," said the bartender hoarsely. "He lives on the high side."

"Every club has an access line. Let me on."

"It ain't the way to get a job."

41 bared his teeth and released the man. "Just let me on."

The bartender shrugged, massaging his throat. He jerked his head toward a doorway half-concealed in the shadows. "Through there."

It could lead to an office. Or it could dump him right outside. 41 walked up to the door, and it slid open for him. He stepped into darkness, blinking to let his eyes adjust. It was an office.

"Lights," he said.

One came on. 41 moved away from the door which had closed behind him. He looked around for communications equipment and found none. Overhead, a cam eye swiveled to follow his movements. 41 stared directly at it.

"I am 41," he said in mercenary code speak. "I want Harva."

As he spoke he drew his pistol and kept it ready in his hand. He turned so that he could keep an eye on the door. He didn't like this small room. It felt like a trap, and it would probably become one if Harva refused to remember him.

A panel in the wall slid open, making him jump. It revealed a viewscreen, which flickered to life. Harva's face, so weathered and wrinkled his features had become indistinct, peered at 41 through one eye. The other empty socket had been fitted with a memory enhancer and sealed with smooth skin. It was said that Harva kept all of his business records filed in the enhancer. Empty his eye and you would have his empire.

"Well, well," said Harva's voice. Thin and ascerbic, it could crack reprimands like a whip or quaver with sentimental emotion. "I always said you would come back to me. Found freelancing poor work, didn't you? If you'd stayed with me, you'd be rich by now."

"I am not poor," said 41.

Harva's laugh cackled over the speakers. His face vanished from the viewscreen and was replaced by a still shot of 41 in his black and silver Hawks uniform.

"Operative 41 of the Allied Intelligence Agency, Special Operations Forces, number 441–41–4041. Rather redundant of you, boy."

41 kept his face expressionless. He had outgrown Harva's games. He had expected Harva's information networks to be current. Dismay was a waste of time.

"So now you're legit. But where's the pretty uniform? Are

you trying to burrow into my organization as an undercover agent? You don't have enough subtlety to be a spy."

"I am not spying," said 41. "I want a favor."

"I owe you nothing," snapped Harva. "I invested fifteen thousand credits training you, and you skipped at the first chance."

"I am not paying debts," said 41. "I want a favor."

"You can't afford my favors, boy."

41 hesitated a moment. Harva probably knew his account balance. Little numbers on a data card had never much interested 41 anyway. He understood barter better. A memory of Kelly's angry face held him only momentarily.

"I have not been erased," he said.

The still shot on the viewscreen was replaced by Harva's face, twisted now with cunning and interest. "Say that again."

"The Hawks erase specialized service knowledge before letting operatives quit," said 41. "They did not erase me."

"You mean," said Harva, and his voice was cracking and quavering, "that you're walking around loose on this planet with your head full of—"

"Yes," said 41. "Are you sure I can't afford a favor?"

Harva's laughter cackled loudly. "My lad, my dear sweet lad, you can afford just about anything you want. Come to Harva. We have much to talk about."

Accommodations on a slaver ship consisted of a dark hold lit only near the door, a bare metal deck to sleep or sit on, just enough heat to maintain minimum body temperature, and a ventilation system inadequate to deal with poor sanitation.

Caesar crouched in the corner he had won for himself and Kelly after several savage fights. His butt was petrified from sitting on metal for so long, but he didn't have anything else to do. If he got up and walked around, someone else would toss Kelly and take the corner. This was the warmest, cleanest spot in the whole stinking hold. Caesar intended to keep it.

Behind him, Kelly moaned and stirred but did not awaken. Carefully Caesar felt in his pockets for the drug patches. He had four left. He didn't know if they would last until the ship reached Kenszana, but if they didn't and the guards figured out Kelly was damaged, that would be the end of his boss. Caesar had seen two slaves injured in the jump to time distort. They had been jettisoned into space and written off as a straight loss.

Junk-heads, however, were treated with more tolerance. As long as they moved and functioned, they were left alone. Caesar figured a place that concentrated on harvesting and exporting drugs wouldn't mind workers that had a few dependency problems.

Their contact had been right about that.

Caesar sighed, worrying. He was nicked up and bruised pretty bad from fighting, but so far he'd passed inspection. His wrist ached from the slave band fused to his flesh. His skin still crawled every time he thought about being strapped to that conveyor belt and run through the sonic scanner for implants and snoops.

Someone at the far end was coughing again, a wracking horrible sound as though his guts were coming up. Beaulieu had loaded Caesar and Kelly with micro-organism protectants, but still Caesar figured that even the most sophisticated protectants had limits.

A hand grabbed him from behind, and Caesar jumped violently.

"Caesar?"

It was Kelly's voice, raspy and weak. Caesar let out his breath in a whoosh, telling his thudding heart to calm down.

"Yusus, boss. You nearly put me on the ceiling. I'm going to come out of this trip with white hair. How're you feeling?"

Kelly was an indistinct shadow in the gloom. He mumbled something Caesar couldn't hear. Caesar groped for Kelly's hand and gripped it. Hot again. The fever came back every time a drug patch started to wear out.

"Thirsty," said Kelly.

"Yo, boss. I hear you," said Caesar. "They'll be bringing food soon. You feel like sitting up? I'll have to leave you to guard our spot here while I get the food. Okay? Think you can do that?"

"Yeah. I can do that."

Caesar gently pulled him up to a sitting position and leaned him against the wall. "Just rest now. Take it easy. How're the shoulders?"

Kelly flinched from his touch. "Okay."

"Yeah, okay like this is a pleasure cruise," muttered Caesar. Their contact had sealed the wounds so they didn't show, but

whatever poison that winged vampire thing had injected into
Kelly was still working on his system. Caesar felt guilty about
that. He'd been the one to get mesmerized, in spite of Kelly's
warnings not to look the thing in the eye. Otherwise, they'd
have both been sitting pretty, ready to take on the drug lords of
Kenszana as soon as they arrived.

Well, he could go throw himself out the jettison hatch or he
could try to make it up to the boss somehow.

How? asked a sarcastic little voice inside his mind. *By
making Kelly an addict*?

A shudder ran through the ship. Over the door a red light
began to flash a warning.

Caesar stared at it in dismay. A lump filled his throat, and he
choked instead of swallowing. "Hey, hey," he said, trying to
keep his voice light and failing. "Guess what? We've arrived.
Country club accommodations coming up. You ready for a
bath, boss?"

"I'd rather have a drink."

"Yo, I hear that," muttered Caesar. Straight rye whiskey,
about two gallons of it. He kept having this feeling that the
hard part was just ahead. He was scared, and making a go of
getting through this alive was up to him, not Kelly.

The slam came then, driving all thought from him. He
groaned as the tremendous g-forces pressed him into the deck,
turning his bones and flesh to jelly, squashing him smaller and
smaller, leaving no room for breathing, blood circulation, or
speech. He wanted to scream. His skull was going to explode
at any moment. He was going to be sick. He was going to black
out.

The ship lurched, bouncing him hard on the deck. It
shuddered, swerved roughly, and sent him tumbling into Kelly,
then slowed velocity. Her ancient bulkheads wheezed in sub
distort speeds, making her sound like she would come apart at
any moment.

Groggy, Caesar slowly pushed himself upright and sat there
with his throbbing head cradled in his hands. No gravity
buffers on this old crate. Nothing to help a body adjust to
breaking the laws of physics. Abruptly he rolled onto his
stomach and was sick.

When he recovered a bit and sat grimacing at the bitter
aftertaste of bile, Kelly put a hand on his shoulder.

"We've got a lot to do, Caesar."

"I know, boss. We'll get there one step at a time. First priority is staying alive. Remember now, you've got to look healthy. Think you can walk out of here?"

Kelly was silent a while, then he said in a low voice filled with shame and need, "Yes, if I have a little help."

Caesar winced, hating that tone. He wanted to hit Kelly, shout at him, put him on straight withdrawal now before it was too late. "You got to get off this stuff. It'll burn you up. You know that."

"I know," said Kelly. "But not till I'm on the planet. I need to look good until we're on the worker line. You know I need to look good."

"Yeah, I know! You don't have to beg for it." Caesar realized he was shouting and forced his voice lower, drawing in a couple of ragged breaths as he tried to regain control. "Just don't beg."

"All right," said Kelly humbly.

That humbleness sprang from the knowledge that Caesar was his source. Caesar rubbed his eyes, feeling as though he were trapped in a nightmare.

Rumbles went through the ship. Caesar knew it was entering orbit, changing velocity, extending its solar panels for auxiliary power storage. They wouldn't get fed now. Too bad. His stomach was rumbling on its own.

The access door to the hold dilated open. Light spilled deep into the darkness of the hold. The slaves cringed with hands over their eyes, scuttling back like insects away from the light.

"Everyone, get up and form two lines!" shouted a voice. "Hurry!"

Caesar climbed stiffly to his feet and pulled Kelly up.

Kelly swayed against him, then steadied himself. "I'll do it," he said.

Caesar hesitated, then swore to himself. Swiftly he peeled off the spent patch behind Kelly's ear and applied a fresh one. Kelly closed his eyes, his face gaunt and beard stubbled. Caesar heard the rhythm of Kelly's breathing change as the drug took hold.

Kelly rubbed his face and straightened, looking more alert, looking more like the capable commander Caesar knew. "Let's get in line, Samms," he said.

How long would it last? Caesar wondered as he complied. Eight hours? Six? Less? Tapo created heavy dependence quickly, especially when there was no mental rejection for it to work against as a balance. Three patches to go. Then the boss fell apart, went into screaming delirium and withdrawal, maybe saw everyone around him turn into gigantic spiders, maybe got violent, maybe got himself killed.

"Don't look so glum," said Kelly. "We can handle this."

"Yo," said Caesar. "I can't wait."

6

The moment he staggered off the shuttle transport onto land, Kelly squinted up at the bright haze obscuring the sun and knew he hated Kenszana. It stank of rot. The ground was a soggy mixture of decomposing leaves and soured mud. Plant life flourished in a jungle of gigantic trees, thick undergrowth, and twisting vines. High heat and humidity levels made sweat break out across Kelly's body. Within seconds, his clothes were plastered to his skin.

Guards shoved them into a ragged line. Kelly and Caesar stood shoulder to shoulder. Kelly was aware of Caesar's sidelong glances at him, but he didn't acknowledge Caesar's worry. Kelly was too busy being angry at himself. It was his fault Caesar's attention was on him instead of the job at hand. He would have to rectify that soon.

He scanned the compound, which was located in a clearing roughly circular in shape. The compound was portable, capable of being shifted to follow the rostma harvest. Large quick-set barracks housed the laborers and guards. In the center of the compound stood the refinery built of three modular units hooked together. It had its own tow-tractors swathed with tarps for rain protection.

Force walls powered by a series of powerful generators on grav-flats surrounded the compound. Kelly glanced at the sky. This time he realized that part of the haze came from a scramble net being beamed across the top of the force walls. He swallowed and frowned. This place was sealed up nice and secure.

Guards shuffled the new laborers into gangs of fifty and unlocked their fusion shackles so that they could move their arms and legs. Five guards per gang made for tight supervision. The guards were clean, alert, and well-trained. No junk-heads among them. They carried plasma rifles, electric prods for shirkers, and comms that kept them linked to each other across the swamp. Belt powerpacks supplied floaters strapped to their boots, so that they could hover, dry-footed, over any part of the water to maintain supervision.

Some of them were hovering now above the muddy tracks between the buildings. Crushed gravel had been poured out in an effort to keep the place from becoming a hopeless bog, but the ground was so saturated with water that nothing had much effect. The jungle itself cocooned the force walls, writhing in constant growth and decay, green shoots and vines hanging with withered tips from contact with the energy barrier.

There was some activity in the area of the refinery, but on the whole the compound looked deserted. The labor crews were all out harvesting, of course.

Kelly frowned. His senses were all triply alert, observing, judging, considering the layout and security measures of the compound. Beyond the barracks stood three smaller quick-sets. Individual quarters, no doubt. One of them had guards standing in front of it. That had to be where Cassandra Caliban was being held. Kelly felt a leap of excitement.

"Caesar," he said softly. "Look at the small quick-sets."

Scratching himself and yawning, Caesar casually turned his gaze in that direction. "Yo ho. I see. Well, now, I guess we've got to—"

A rifle butt slammed Caesar to the ground. "No talking!"

Caesar writhed in the mud, gasping with pain. Kelly started to kneel beside him, but the guard aimed his weapon at Kelly's midsection. Kelly froze where he was.

The guard kicked Caesar. "Get up."

Another guard was going down the row, assigning each laborer a number. Kelly received 85, Caesar 86.

Groaning a bit, Caesar staggered to his feet and stood hunched, still clutching his stomach. "Yusus," he whispered. "41 would feel right at home."

The guard whirled and drew a knife. "The penalty for talking without permission is to have your tongue cut out."

He advanced on Caesar, who turned white and took a step back. Alarm went through Kelly. He knew that Caesar would fight and Caesar would die, right here and now.

Swiftly Kelly stepped between Caesar and the guard. "It's my fault," he said, looking the furious guard in the eye. "He's my supplier. I was trying to—"

The guard backhanded Kelly across the jaw, sending him staggering. "Shut up!"

"What's the problem here?" said an incisive voice.

The guard whirled at once. "No problem, Mr. Frant."

Flexing his jaw, Kelly looked around.

Frant was of medium height, built well and compact. He was of earthstock, but drug usage, radiation exposure, or genetic tampering had given him platinum-white hair and lavender eyes. His face was clean-shaven, and he had the slight puffiness along the jaw that indicated UV-block injections. Goggles and an air filter mask were slung about his neck. His coveralls were beautifully creased in spite of the heat, and his boots had hardly any mud on them.

"You're sure there's no trouble here, Orson?"

The guard came to attention. "Just disciplining these new workers, Mr. Frant. They don't understand the rules."

"Rules!" began Caesar hotly. "There's no—"

Kelly tapped Caesar's wrist in a warning to be quiet. Frant noticed. His lavender eyes bored into Kelly's. He had the look of a man who missed very little.

"I was just about to cut out this red-head's tongue, Mr. Frant," said Orson. "That's all. He ought to be clipped in the hamstrings too. He's a troublemaker. As for this tall pal of his—"

"Yes," said Frant and the guard fell silent. Frant held out his hand and Orson gave him the list. "Numbers 85 and 86. Bought on Methanus. Not the usual stock we get from there."

"You want me to check the invoices, Mr. Frant?" said Orson.

Frant glanced briefly at a tall woman standing silently behind him. "Elga will do that."

Without a word Elga pulled out a hand computer and began punching access numbers. Kelly's nerves tightened. Too careful a check could perhaps find a discrepancy, could perhaps arouse suspicion. Why couldn't Caesar keep his mouth shut for once?

"You're angry, 85," said Frant. "Angry at 86. Why? Because he's gotten you in trouble with him? Or because he's failed to carry out his orders?"

Kelly stiffened. For the first time he felt a cold dash of fear. Was this man a telepath?

"He's my supplier," said Kelly, aware of a burst of shame. More than anything he wanted to stand straight, look this Frant in the eye, and show him they were equal in wit and ability. He didn't want to cringe or admit the need crawling in his veins. But he knew the tapo had given him the best cover he could possibly have here. "If you waste him, at least give me the patches he has in his pockets."

Frant frowned. "Search them both."

Rough hands slapped over Kelly and Caesar. Scanners beeped loudly at Caesar's pocket. Orson pulled out the drug patches, plus a data card and a thin holo of a woman's face.

"Hey!" he said angrily. "These are mine! You picked my pockets, you little bastard."

His vicious punch sent Caesar sprawling into another laborer. Both of them fell, and Caesar didn't get up.

Kelly flinched inside, furious and doing his best not to show anything. Frant was still watching him, testing him, judging. Kelly gritted his teeth and stared at the ground.

Orson kicked Caesar. "Damned thief. I'll—"

"That's enough," said Frant quietly.

Orson halted with a scowl of reluctance, his breath huffing.

"Clear this line of workers," said Frant. "We didn't buy an extra two shifts to have them stand around idle. Get them geared and ready to go out. Elga will show you the location I want harvested this afternoon. Take 86 with them. And, Orson?"

"Yes, Mr. Frant?"

"No mutilations. We're running short of quota already. If 86 remains a discipline problem after a few days of work, we'll discuss what to do with him. Is that clear?"

Orson's small eyes glowered. "Yes, Mr. Frant."

Frant stepped aside and gestured at another guard. "Cut 85 out and take him to the lab."

Kelly glanced sharply at him. He didn't like the sound of this at all. But he made himself say eagerly, "Does this mean specialized work? I'm good at that sort of thing. Indoor work, I mean."

"I'm sure you are," said Frant dryly, not fooled. He smiled, but the expression did not reach his eyes. "No, we're going to let Elga take you apart. I know military when I see it."

Kelly's mouth went dry. "You're wrong."

Frant turned away with a gesture. "To the lab."

Two guards closed in on Kelly and seized him by the arms. As he walked away between them Kelly could not help glancing back at Caesar, now being shaken awake. Frant was still watching. He smiled as though Kelly had confirmed his suspicions. Angrily Kelly whipped his head forward.

Everything was going wrong.

Elga was Boxcan, extremely tall and strong but awkward, as though all her joints were too loosely put together. Her face looked like a primitive stone carving, with a slab-like brow shelf, narrow oblong eyes, a flat triangular nose, and a blunt jaw. Like most Boxcans she moved with slow, heavy competence. There was nothing quick, light, or graceful about her. No animation lightened her serious expression. Her eyes were neither hostile like Orson's nor shrewd like Frant's. She simply used them to observe Kelly.

The laboratory Kelly was taken to was located in one of the three modular units of the refinery. The guards put Kelly inside a narrow cubicle just large enough to hold a restraint chair, a large scanner unit, and a computer desk. As soon as his fusion shackles were locked to the arms of the chair, the guards left.

Elga closed the door, muffling the rhythmic booming of refinery machinery. Kelly forced himself to sit quietly, but the palms of his hands were sweating. She can't find anything, he kept reminding himself. But he remained nervous just the same.

"What did Frant mean about taking me apart?" he asked.

Elga looked up from the data sheet she was carefully filling out. "He is Mr. Frant to you."

Her voice was slow, like the rest of her, and loud. She wasn't shouting. Her large lung size gave her a lot of voice.

"All right, so I call him Mr. Frant," said Kelly. "Why have I been brought here? What are you going to do to me?"

"You can stop acting, 85. You are a highly trained military operative. It is not necessary to pretend to be a coward. We have observed otherwise."

Damn. Kelly gnawed on his lower lip. His earlier keenness of wit was wearing off. He felt tired and thirsty. A shiver ran through him.

"All right," he said finally. "I've been in Fleet service. A long time ago. What about it? I'm not in it now. I wouldn't be here if—"

"You are a spy," she said with finality. "I shall prove it." But she didn't.

The hum of the scanner filled the tiny room. Its power and degree of sophistication surpassed the one used on Kelly and Caesar on Methanus. Had he still been wearing his translator and standard implants, they would have been detected. He was afraid as Elga ran the scanner over him a second time, and a third—each time switching to a higher level of intensity—that this machinery would detect his transponder. It was microscopic in size and located on the basal level of his skin on the inside of his right upper arm. It pulsed one beat per seventy-nine seconds on a neutrino wavelength and required a highly specialized receiver specifically attuned to its frequency to pick it up. Kelly kept telling himself that they would have caught identical transponders in Ambassador Caliban and her staff if they had equipment that good. But he worried just the same as Elga took a fourth scan, this one tuned to such intensity his nerves itched as it passed over him.

"There's nothing!" he said before he could stop the words. "You've found nothing. I'm not a spy."

Reluctantly she switched off the scanner. Kelly sagged in his chair with relief. He was sweating again, drenched in moisture. His muscles had cramped from tension. For a moment he closed his eyes. They felt hot behind his eyelids. The itching in his nerves did not let up, however. Instead, it was getting worse. He twitched, forcing open his eyes with an effort. He couldn't need another patch yet. It was too soon. He must not think about it.

The door opened and Frant entered. There really wasn't enough room for both him and Elga. They towered over Kelly, making him feel as though he were at the wrong end of a fish-eye lens.

"He's been wired lightly and fitted for various implants," said Elga. "They were recently removed."

"How recently?" asked Frant.

She shrugged. "Precision is not possible."

Frant's eyes were darker indoors. They looked like amethysts now as they probed Kelly. "When were your implants removed?"

Kelly pulled himself together. "A few weeks ago. Maybe two months. I don't remember exactly."

Frant struck him. It was a light blow, yet numbing pain jolted Kelly from his mouth to the top of his head. He realized, as soon as his ears stopped ringing, that Frant's hand was metal. Fear balled up in the pit of Kelly's stomach before he could control it. Now he knew why Frant had purple eyes. He did *not* want to tangle with a cyborg.

"You will answer my question truthfully," said Frant.

Gingerly Kelly ran his tongue over his molars, checking them, then probed his cut and swelling lip. He spat some blood on the floor.

Frant's eyes narrowed. He lifted his hand to strike again. But before he could do so, Kelly switched tactics.

"You don't have to pulp me," he said. "I'll talk."

Frant lowered his hand. "Do so."

"Are you augmented with lie detectors?" asked Kelly.

"Yes."

Kelly sighed. "The implants came out twenty-seven days ago, nine hours, and a few odd minutes. I am—was—a commander in the Space Fleet. Ground communications operations. They busted me for letting independents carry piggy-back communications. It was always light traffic, never any security risks. I don't see why I shouldn't supplement the measly pay—"

"What is your name?" asked Frant.

He was concentrating. His eyes had a distant look as though he were listening to other information.

"My name is Jordan Carstairs," said Kelly. "Commander Jordan Carstairs."

"What are you doing here?"

Kelly tried to laugh, but it sounded pretty hollow. "I keep asking myself that. Look, Frant, maybe we can work a deal. I was broken in rank, facing charges, my pay suspended, my possessions confiscated for debt payments. I couldn't face a trial so I ran for it. But the creep who was supposed to get me off Earth shanghaied me. The next thing I know, I'm on Methanus being sold to the highest bidder. I don't want to spend the rest of my life digging in the mud. I can do things for you, Frant. I can—"

"Shut up," said Frant.

There was enough menace in his voice to warn Kelly. He fell silent, trying to breathe normally instead of in ragged bursts. His training to fool lie detectors had been thorough, but it was never one hundred percent foolproof. One slip of tonality, and the detector would register it. Frant was probably equipped with top grade, doubly sensitive equipment.

Kelly studied him anxiously, but Frant's face gave nothing away.

"How long have you had your habit?" asked Frant.

Kelly's tension eased fractionally. It was working. "It's not a habit," he said with enough shrillness to set off Frant's detector. "Just a social thing. I'm not really hooked. I got it from a doctor back—back when I was ill. I had to keep working. Couldn't afford to let a substitute see my system, so I took tapo. You know, the drug that takes away all those bad feelings? I mean, you feel so good you don't even know you're sick. That's all. I'm not some common junk-head."

Without warning Frant toed the lever that released Kelly's shackles. Frant seized him by the shoulders and yanked him half out of the chair. He shoved Kelly's face close to the mirrored steel side of the scanner.

"Look at yourself. I see a junk-head. What do you see, Commander?"

Kelly frowned at his reflection, momentarily forgetting his role in his shock. He knew he could not look exactly chipper, but he didn't expect the bloodshot, red-rimmed eyes, the gaunt

sallowness of his skin beneath ugly beard stubble, or the visible
tremor of his lips. He looked like something that had been
living in the gutter for a year or two.

Appalled, Kelly placed his hand on the scanner, covering his
reflection. He hadn't expected tapo to tear him down so fast.
He didn't know much about the drug, except for its ability to
mask augmentation rejection so that people wired with exten-
sive bio-wave could continue to function at their high-paying
jobs. Unlike rostma, tapo was an upper-class drug, used often
by professionals who believed, as Kelly had himself casually
thought, that the habit could be kicked easily at any time. He'd
been telling himself that Beaulieu could pull him out as soon as
he got back, to not worry about it, to not let it get in his way.
Now he wondered what he had gotten himself into.

Could he get back? Was there a point where sacrifice for the
job became too high?

Frant's grip on his shoulder stirred up the pain of his
wounds. Kelly winced and tried to draw free. Frant shoved him
back to the chair.

"You are very, very good," said Frant. "You act well. Your
voice is pathetic, stupidly confident, arrogant, afraid—all the
right tones. You have been well taught. My detector registers
no insincerities beyond the obvious ones. It tells me you are
exactly what you claim to be—a foolish officer stuck in a
dead-end career, troubled by an expensive drug habit, and
skimming profits to support a lifestyle otherwise beyond your
means. It is an excellent cover."

"I—"

Frant held up his hand. "Please, Commander. I am sure that
if I had Elga go to all the trouble of infiltrating Fleet database
records and personnel files, she would find Jordan Carstairs
with all of his documentation, along with a record of his court
martial in abstentia and a warrant for his arrest. It would be
very convincing."

"It's true," said Kelly desperately, and now he wasn't
having to act much. What had given him away? he wondered.
How the hell was he going to pull this off? "I'm not cut out for
slave labor. I can help you in other ways. There must be
something I can do to earn my way out of this. Please. I—"

"Your begging is amusing," said Frant without a smile.
"But I have other things to do besides watch you enact this play

of yours. You will work here, Commander Kelly. But it will
not earn a way out for you."

Kelly froze. For a moment he was certain his own nerves
had made him hear wrong. Frant could not know him. There
was not the remotest chance of it.

"You are Commander Bryan Kelly of Special Operations.
You are here, along with your men, to rescue the Zoan
ambassador. Whether you are very brave or merely stupid to
try such a thing does not matter. We know who you are. We
have been expecting this attempt for days. Welcome to
Kenszana, Kelly."

Kelly's ears were roaring so loudly he almost could not hear
Frant. Who had betrayed him? 41? The idea hurt so much it
was like a cramp in his stomach. He wanted to deny it, to
convince himself that he had not misjudged 41, that their
friendship had been real, would last even now.

But who else would do it?

The mission was over, a failure. He and Caesar were
finished. And within a matter of hours Beaulieu, Mohatsa, and
Siggerson would be coming here into a trap. There was nothing
Kelly could do to help them. There was nothing he could do to
help himself.

He stared bleakly at Frant, making no effort to deny
anything. "What happens now?"

Frant smiled and opened the door. "You work, 85. You
work here on Kenszana and harvest rostma for us until you die
of drug withdrawal or foot rot infection. We paid money for
you. We shall have you earn it."

The guard came in past Frant. Kelly rose to his feet, feeling
shaky, hot, and sick.

"Who?" he said. "Who betrayed us?"

"That," said Frant coldly, " is none of your business. Get
him out of here."

7

Cassandra stood at the grimy window of her quarters and watched a pair of guards escorting a tall, black-haired man across the compound. She sighed, loathing the sight of one more laborer as much as she loathed this place and all the suffering and degradation it fostered. Somehow, she had to get out of here. She could not depend upon rescue. That would have happened days ago if it was going to happen at all. Her worry that Zoe would muster some kind of motley flotilla and come in to be anniliated for her sake had faded. Now she feared the government was giving in to whatever demands had been made for her return. She did not want to think she was worth that.

Most of all, however, she resented being a pawn in a game of power and coercion. She did not intend to continue being one for long.

The black-haired man was tall and well-built. He carried himself with an athletic, almost angry stride. Her interest was caught by the alert set of his head and the way he kept looking at her quick-set.

For a moment hope rose within her. Perhaps she was wrong about there being no rescue. This man didn't shuffle along like the other slaves, hopeless and beaten into submission. But he was too tall for a Zoan. Perhaps the Alliance had sent him? She stepped closer to the window, rubbing it although the grime was on the outside. She wanted a better look at him.

But then one of the guards struck the black-haired man, who sagged between them. They shook him and struck him again with their usual brutality. Cassandra wanted to close her eyes and turn away, but she forced herself to go on watching. She wanted every cruelty, every barbarism she had witnessed since coming here to be imprinted upon her memory forever. The rostma harvesting on Kenszana must be stopped. And if she survived this, she meant to use every means at her disposal to put an end to it.

The guards dragged the man away, and Cassandra left the window. He was not her rescuer, but just another victim.

She circled her small quarters, so painfully bare yet far from inhumane. She had a bed, a chair and table, a window, and good ventilation. She was fed regularly and not abused. Frant visited her once a day for never longer than five minutes at a time. He stuck to inquiries about her needs or wants.

Being well-treated only made the situation around her worse. She did not want to be singled out as special and kept like precious contraband, while her staff was out there being beaten and ill-used. She had seen Thessic once as he crossed the compound in a line of workers shackled together. His small shoulders were bent with weariness. He was coated from head to foot in gray mud. He could barely walk for exhaustion. Little Thessic who had a mind like a computer and whose obsession with fashion and neatness made some criticize him for dandyism. She needed his analytical mind now to help her work a way out of this dilemma.

As for Jon and Janitte, she had seen neither of them. She feared they were dead.

If she ever dared give way to her emotions, she would cry forever. So she permitted herself no tears at all. She could not afford to crack under the strain she'd undergone since their abduction by the Jostic raiders. She had to find a way out.

Even if she got lost in the swamp and perished there, at least she would no longer be a bargaining chip for the Mechtaxlan Cartel. Robbing them of their leverage had to be her first priority.

She circled her quarters again, thinking. There was only one door and two guards stood sentry at all times. The window was on the same wall as the door. She had no weapon and nothing that she could convert into one. If she attempted to simply dash outside past Frant when he came, she would be easily caught.

A rapping on the door pulled her from her thoughts. She looked up, her breath coming up short in her throat.

"Yes?" she said.

The door opened and Frant stood there, looking as crisp and competent as ever. He missed nothing with those peculiar eyes.

Anxious that he should not guess her intentions, she tried to master her expression and failed.

Frant stepped inside. "You're upset. What's wrong?"

She thought fast and decided it was now or never. "I'm bored!" she said angrily. "I've been stuck in this chicken crate for days. My whole body is getting stiff from atrophy."

"Elga will come and give you conversation when her duty shift is over," he said.

"No! I don't want conversation. I want exercise. Some fresh air."

He looked amused. "Fresh air on Kenszana?"

She wanted to throw something at him to wipe off that smile. That's when she realized her anger wasn't just pretense. Rage and resentment were boiling inside her, no longer as bottled and controlled as she wanted her emotions to be.

Her father had told her to never act on raw emotion, but to think things through first. Now, however, she could not follow that advice. If she kept herself clear-headed and rational, she wouldn't act at all.

"You are mocking me," she said, glaring at Frant. "Why do you bother to come and ask me what I want, if you never give me anything I ask for? Is it a game you're playing to remind me of how helpless I am?"

"You are kept hidden in this hut for reasons you need not know."

"Kept in here while my staff is abused. Why am I treated differently than they?"

Frant's smile faded. "You know why. Don't pretend to be a fool, Ambassador."

"May I at least go for a walk? This place is sealed. Guards are everywhere. I can't exactly jump the force wall."

"No. I must refuse your request."

"Why?"

"If you move your table beneath the window, that will leave plenty of room for you to do calisthenics."

"I hate calisthenics," she said, trying to mask her rising desperation with anger. "I want to take a walk."

Frant stepped back through the doorway. "Your food will arrive in thirty minutes."

The door closed before she could make one last appeal. Furious, she kicked it.

So much for exploring the compound in search of a way out. Damn Frant and his caution.

She shoved the table beneath the window, slamming it against the wall so that the flimsy construction of the building shuddered. The roof overhead creaked. She looked up, her disappointment fading enough for her to think again.

There was no ceiling. Just the support ribs and the links where the three sections of the quick-set snapped together. If she unsnapped those links, could she get out through the top?

It was worth investigating.

The *Sabre* came roaring into the Stevolian System at time distort 8. As she passed the outermost of the system's twelve planets, the ship cut speed to sublight and switched on her waver shield so that she vanished completely, leaving only the vaguest ripple of distortion that could not be detected in the gravitational fields among the planets.

She also activated a full-sized hologram of a battered old smuggler ship obviously converted from a freighter by having two-thirds of her hold lopped off and massive engine thrusters bolted onto her stern. This hologram was projected ahead of the *Sabre* so that it appeared to coast on its impetus through the spectacular rings of the sixth planet before shifting course for an approach to Kenszana. Their objective shimmered green and silver against the blackness of space: beauty with a core of rot. Two small moons spun around it. One of them originated a security scan.

Slowing to one-quarter pulse, the *Sabre*'s communications system emitted a password signal bought at a high price off the black market. It wasn't the most recent signal, but it was accepted by Kenszana's defense system.

The hologram passed through the defense zone followed by the *Sabre* wrapped in her waver shield like a ghost. They had to jockey space with a pair of needle-thin scoutships bearing the Mechtaxlan logo and a real smuggler ship.

"Locking into orbit," said Siggerson aloud to the empty bridge. He finished settling the *Sabre* into a geosynchronous pattern, close in at twenty-thousand kilometers, and went to work on boosting power to the holo projectors.

The main worry had been that once they were in orbit, the planet would tend to show through the hologram. Two extra projectors had been aligned with the other three usually required to make a realistic, fully dimensional holo. The *Sabre* was too new and too technologically advanced to be disguised as a smuggler. An old, emptied-out wreck couldn't be towed at high distort speeds. The holo was the only way they could look like authentic smugglers without sacrificing all the ship's capabilities they needed.

Siggerson had done most of the redesigning of the projectors, and he was proud of the results now as he tested the projection one last time. It was holding beautifully.

"Non-operational lighting," he said and the overhead illumination brightened from the dim setting designed to enhance his digital board readouts. "Cancel astrogation screen."

It faded and Siggerson set the automateds to take over for him.

Leaning back in his chair, he stretched until his joints creaked, then nudged Ouoji with his toe to awaken her. She was curled up in a rumpled knot of gray fur, asleep as usual. When he touched her, she lifted her head and blinked round blue eyes. Her ear flaps opened slightly, giving her a comical look of inquiry.

"We're here," he said. "No one else even bothered to come to the bridge to watch us go through the system when I announced slam. Even you slept through all the scenery."

Ouoji yawned and put her head back down upon her paws. Rebuffed, Siggerson frowned and left his master station. The squad was coming apart with Kelly gone. 41's desertion should have been reported to the AIA immediately. Failure to report him was a breach of regulations that could result in arrest and charges for all of them. Siggerson grimaced to himself as he took the lift down to the mess lounge. Camaraderie and esprit de corps were all very well, but they should not serve as an excuse to cover 41 from the law.

The lift doors opened, and a battering ram struck him in the center of the forehead, exploding his skull with pain. He staggered backward, and blackness engulfed him.

The jolt of hitting the floor brought him partway back to consciousness. He felt himself being dragged by the feet. He wanted very much to open his eyes and see who had hit him, but the blackness was like quicksand. He sank into it again.

Sticky, awful taste on tongue. Something stuck to face. Jaws forced open. Mouth too dry. Swallowing difficult. Something in mouth. Tastes worse than . . .

Siggerson came to for the second time and realized he was gagged with fibrous repair tape, the stuff used to bind split tubing in the coolant sections of the ventilation system before adhesive was sprayed over it.

He managed to open his eyes. At once he regretted it, for light seared his eyeballs and made them throb sharply with pain. He blinked and squinted, but the light went on blinding him and making his eyes water. Finally his eyes adjusted, and he almost wished they hadn't.

Phila lay on the floor near his feet. She was prone with her face turned away from him. Her hands were bound with tape behind her back and there was something crumpled about the way she lay there, something too still.

Siggerson frowned. He was having difficulty breathing, and worry about Phila shortened his breath a little more. He could smell blood, and a sudden rush through his nostrils made him realize his nose was bleeding. He choked, struggling to breathe. Although his hands were bound behind him, he used them and managed to scoot himself up to a sitting position. He leaned against the wall, panting.

His head began to ache horribly, with jagged splinters of pain that jabbed around his eye sockets into his cheekbones. The light overhead pulsed through his pupils. He wanted to crawl off into darkness, but he had to think, had to figure out what had happened and what he was going to do next.

With a lot of wriggling, straining, cursing, and twisting himself into a knot, he finally succeeded in scooting his bound hands beneath his buttocks, then his thighs. He rested, sweat drenching him, then he worked until he had his feet slid through and his hands were resting in his lap.

Wiping some of the blood from his face with the back of his knuckles, he worked off the gag. The relief was overwhelming.

"Phila," he said hoarsely.

He hobbled on his knees to her side and bent over her. His fingers found her pulse beating erratically and fast. Blood oozed from behind her ear, matting her dark hair. She did not stir when he spoke her name again.

Siggerson went to work on freeing his hands. Pulling on the tape stretched it, making it thinner but tougher and less flexible. He could not reach the end of it with his fingers. Using his teeth was slow work. He needed Ouoji to gnaw through it, but for all he knew she was either still sleeping lazily on the bridge, or she had been clubbed as well and possibly jettisoned through the garbage chute.

He had no doubt Nash was the attacker. But what the Zoan hoped to gain by hurting his allies, Siggerson could not begin to guess.

By the time he worked his hands free, his wrists were swollen and chafed raw. He flung the bits of tape away and staggered to his feet. The effort involved brought on an intensified throbbing in his skull, making it feel as though it was going to split in half at any moment. He gasped and supported himself on the wall for a moment, waiting until the worst faded marginally enough for him to function. Gingerly he touched his forehead and winced. A large bump had swelled there. It was extremely painful to the touch.

The world looked a little crooked. It didn't matter. He had to find Beaulieu before Nash took her out as well.

His slow, tottery search finally located Beaulieu stashed unconscious on deck three in an engine-access ladder well. The black woman was already in her undercover costume of a short, sleeveless jerkin that barely laced together across her breasts and left part of her midriff bare. Her trousers were skin-tight leather, dyed a rich purple, and she wore boots to match. A thin metallic cord was tied around each of her biceps, where amulets of small bones dangled. Siggerson hoped they were synthetic. She had oiled her skin so that it glistened, enchancing every slight ripple of muscle. Her hair had been shaved to the scalp on each side, leaving a miniature mohawk dyed in bands of gold and purple. A gold metallic headband and a sinister-looking symbol painted on her left cheek made her look, to Siggerson, completely ridiculous. She was a medical scientist; she belonged in a lab, not in cloak and dagger games.

Siggerson dragged her from the ladder well. She stirred, striking out wildly, then sat up with her eyes wide open.

Siggerson grabbed her arms. "Easy, Antoinette."

Her gaze focused on him and grew less wild. "Oh, God," she said in a moan and rubbed her face. "I walked into the teleport bay and the roof caved in. Who hit me?"

"Nash. He got Phila and me. I haven't tracked him down yet."

"Oh." Beaulieu was still wandering. With a visible effort she tried to pull herself together. "You look like hell. Are you having trouble seeing? Hearing? How's your sense of balance?"

"I'm fine," lied Siggerson. "I don't know about Mohatsa, however. How did Nash get loose? I thought he was confined to quarters."

"He was. Phila coded the lock herself. I guess he figured out a way to override it." She frowned and pressed the heels of her palms against her eyes. "Where is Phila?"

"Never mind her," said Siggerson. "We must go to the armory. Then we have to contain Nash before he accomplishes his objective."

"I thought he was on our side," said Beaulieu.

Siggerson helped her to her feet, but she seemed already recovered. He wished he was. Nausea shifted in the pit of his stomach. He swallowed uneasily.

"Nash is on the side of the Zoans," said Siggerson. "Apparently he's decided that Alliance help isn't good enough. Come on. Let's get armed."

"You need treatment—"

"I'll keep. We have work to do."

Eight minutes later they entered the armory. Crawling up emergency ladders had left Siggerson winded and weak, his head throbbing worse than ever, but he did not want lift activity to betray the fact that they were free.

While Beaulieu hustled around the racks, selecting weapons, Siggerson decoded the lock on the small emergency hatchway leading into a minuscule auxiliary master station. He crawled inside and had to duck because there wasn't enough clearance for his height. The only light was that coming from the armory; it wasn't quite enough. He groped cautiously for the security scanner and pressed his palm flat against it.

The screen was cold against his skin, but it quickly warmed to match his body temperature. A blue scanning band oscillated across the screen, casting a cold, eerie light around the silhouette of his splayed fingers.

"Siggerson, Olaf," he said. "Pilot, MSS *Sabre*. IDent number 555–96–0021. Classified suffix number 476."

"Voice print verified. Palm print and IDent codes verified. Security lock released."

"Cancel duality link between bridge and auxiliary master stations," said Siggerson hastily, anxious that no activity in here show on the bridge. He didn't want Nash pinpointing them. "Auxiliary reserve power only."

"Acknowledged," said the computer.

The control boards powered up around him. As long as they were running off battery power instead of the photonic drive, no power rerouting would show either.

Beaulieu stuck her head through the hatchway. "Found him yet?"

"Just a moment, Doctor. Computer, conduct internal ship scan. Locate all human lifeforms aboard."

"Working." The computer hummed to itself a moment, then a three-dimensional blueprint of the ship came onscreen. Flashing yellow indicators marked Siggerson and Beaulieu, Mohatsa still where he'd left her, and Nash on the bridge.

Siggerson glanced at Beaulieu. "He's on the bridge. Computer, identify his activity."

"Holographic projection cancelled. Communications channel open for two-way transmissions. Receiving planetary communications signal."

Siggerson slammed his fist upon the edge of the console. "Damn! He's betrayed us to them. That—"

Breaking off his own emotional reaction, Siggerson left his sentence hanging and said quickly, "Computer, put communications channel on audio here."

"Acknowledged."

Seconds later Nash's voice came on: ". . . ship is secured and in my possession. It's ready to be handed over as soon as you give me proper assurances that Ambassador Caliban is still alive. . . ."

"He's selling us to the drug-runners," said Siggerson. Cold fury cleared away his headache. "That idiot is going to hand over this ship for a diplomat? A speech-riddled, pompous, good-for-nothing colonial diplomat? Politicians are as plentiful as sparlin crystals. Anyone could take her place. *Anyone!*"

"Siggerson, calm down," said Beaulieu. "We've got to take him—"

Siggerson wasn't listening. He swept his hand over the controls, placing an override on communications, and cut the channel in the middle of the planetary spokesman's reply. If he'd had the means without jeopardizing all of them, he would have flushed the bridge with lethal gas, purged it of that repellant, short-sighted fool, and jettisoned him with the other garbage.

Beaulieu gripped his sleeve and shook him. "Siggerson, what did you do?"

"I cut the channel. There will be no deal."

Her eyes widened. "You did *what*? Have you lost your mind? You just gave us away. We had the perfect opportunity to slip up to the bridge and take him. Now he's warned. He's going to be hell to get off the bridge once he barricades himself in."

Siggerson stepped out of auxiliary back into the armory. He selected one of the laser-scoped pistols lying on the counter and thumbed its setting to full charge. "I don't care," he said. His anger was like ice, chilling the rest of his emotions, leaving only his mind functioning like a machine, already calculating every move and preparing for it. "He's not giving away this ship."

She muttered something he didn't catch, shaking her head. Siggerson ignored her. Gripping the pistol, he stepped out into the corridor and headed for the bridge.

Unfortunately, the bridge was designed to be defended, not breached. Siggerson had already made sure the doors could not be locked. But Nash would be ready to pick him off as soon as they opened. Siggerson steeled himself, ignoring Beaulieu's steady stream of curses behind him.

The doors slid open. Siggerson ducked and threw himself into an awkward, ill-practiced roll. His own pistol nearly fired because he was gripping it so hard.

But no one shot at him.

Siggerson flattened himself behind a seating bench and listened, his heart hammering in his own ears. He felt dizzy. His rush of adrenaline could not sustain him much longer. When nothing happened, he cautiously raised his head above the bench.

There was no one on the bridge besides himself and Beaulieu, hunched in the doorway with her weapon ready for anything. Then Ouoji came out of hiding, lashing her tail and chittering angrily.

Siggerson climbed wearily to his feet. "Where is he?"

"Probably hiding in the lift," said Beaulieu, nodding at the closed lift door to Siggerson's left. "That's the only other exit. Siggerson, watch out."

But Siggerson did not believe Nash was lurking to ambush them. He hurried to his master station and, sure enough, the teleport light was blinking.

"He's using the teleport!"

Beaulieu ran to him. "Cut power!"

Siggerson's fingers were already racing over the controls. But there was a safety factor built in, designed to prevent an accidental shut off of power during beaming. That hindered him now, and he was so furious he went blank and could not remember the override sequence in time.

"Too late," he said, dropping into his chair. "He's gone."

Beaulieu paced back and forth. "Good riddance. Except—"

"—except," Siggerson finished for her, "he's given us away and ruined our chances of getting the ambassador out of there. As for Kelly—"

The loud buzz of the warning alarm startled him. For an instant he stared without comprehension at the flashing indicators, then he focused and jumped into action.

"What is it?" said Beaulieu.

"The planetary defense system is locking weaponry on us," said Siggerson breathlessly, his fingers flying. "Activating force wall."

"Siggerson, that won't protect us from a planetary defense zone! We've got to get out of here!"

He shook his head, not looking up. "No time. Got to first make sure we—"

The first missiles hit, and it was as though a gigantic hand slammed the ship sideways. Knocked from his chair, Siggerson went tumbling across the floor. The alarms sounded louder than ever. He felt a shudder in the deck and knew a moment of despair. Not this ship. She was a piece of art. If those junkheads so much as cracked her pyrillium hull . . .

The second barrage of missiles hit, and this time Siggerson heard the unmistakable roar of an explosion. Praying that the automateds were sealing the bulkheads, closing off any hull leakage, and executing fire damage control, Siggerson scrambled to his feet and threw himself at the controls. Beaulieu was right; they had to get out of range before they were pounded into splinters.

"Force wall down forty-five percent," said Beaulieu.

Siggerson blinked the sweat from his eyes. He didn't know she could read sensor data, much less translate power configuration curves or calculate percentages.

"We can stand one more hit," he muttered.

It seemed to take forever to slip the *Sabre* off the automateds and resume manual piloting control. But then, with a slight change in her engine ratios, the ship was his, resting poised at the ends of his fingertips.

Without consulting the astrogation screen, he shot her screaming from orbit. Beaulieu lost her balance and crawled to the nearest station chair, where she fitted herself into the restraints. The next barrage of missiles scattered just short of them. Only one glanced off their flank, at quarter blast instead of dead on. It tilted them, but Siggerson boosted speed without bothering much for correction.

They jumped into time distort, which was a crazy thing to do only forty thousand kilometers from a planet, an insane thing to do within moon range, a demented thing to do within a solar system.

They cleared the moons by ten thousand meters, alarms screaming all over the ship, and bounced off the distorted gravitational fields of the next two planets, which they were already approaching too fast—so fast the nearest one loomed across the viewscreen until magnification could adjust no more.

"Siggerson!" screamed Beaulieu.

Sweat poured into his eyes and his skull was splitting so fiercely that he could barely see. Yet he was unaware of either condition as he ran through the calculations rapidly, using his head and guessing at most of it because there wasn't time to access the astrogation computer. It was beeping at him, trying to warn him, but he didn't need a machine to tell him what he already knew.

They were too close and too fast. The whole fabric of space was warped in distort time. Planets weren't where they should be. They were folded into new locations, and navigation required precision not guessing.

He guessed anyway, praying a little although he hadn't really prayed in years. He swung them fourteen degrees in what he hoped was the right direction, and then slammed them to sublight speed. The *Sabre* lurched violently, keeling as though the abuse had knocked out her stabilizers. G-force overwhelmed the straining gravity buffers. Siggerson felt smashed into his chair, and he could smell something burning.

The *Sabre* slowed, still keeling although the indicator that would have told him her hull was breaking up did not flash on. Then she stopped, lights flickering, something still shorting enough to send smoke curling out from behind a panel.

Dazedly Siggerson blinked at the viewscreen, which was readjusting for new distances. The sensors told him they were seventeen thousand kilometers distant from the sixth planet, inside its rings, and far too close to the atmosphere.

Siggerson backed her out. The *Sabre* wallowed, straining against the planet's gravitational pull, but she made it to a safe orbital distance. Switching everything onto standby, Siggerson sat limply in his chair for a moment. He needed to get up and start assessing damage checks, but right now he couldn't move.

He shut his eyes until a gentle touch on his shoulder startled him awake.

"Siggerson?" It was Beaulieu.

He stared up into her face, which held a mixture of concern and appraisal. She was probing the lump on his forehead. He winced and thrust her hand away.

"I'm all right. Got to get after damage control."

"Siggerson."

He moved past her, leaving his chair and straightening carefully. "She'll have to have a hull patch. Did you see her in dry dock? How beautiful she was? Now she's just as nicked and battered as—"

"Siggerson."

Her sharp tone got through to him that time. He paused and glanced at her. "Yes?"

"You got us out of that mess alive," Beaulieu said with a smile. "I don't think any other pilot could have done it."

He almost smiled back, but there wasn't time and their situation was too grave. "Let's not celebrate yet," he said. "We have to go back."

Beaulieu's smile faded. "How are we going to do that?"

"If the waver shield is still working, we can do it easily enough. We won't be able to establish a geosynchronous orbit, however, and still avoid the defense system on that damned moon. That means teleportation will be out of range a certain number of hours each time we go around."

"By now Nash will have given Kelly and Caesar away," said Beaulieu. "They could be already dead."

Siggerson stared at her coldly. "Are you suggesting we abandon them and scrub the mission?"

"No, I'm not, damn you! What a terrible thing to say."

"Then go to Mohatsa and fix her up. She's got to be able to go down with you—"

"And you," said Beaulieu. "You're reporting to sickbay too."

"I'm fine," said Siggerson. "I've told you that before. Get going. We don't have much time to save them."

"I think you've got some damage that needs attention—"

"I'll keep!" he shouted, making his head pound. "Kelly won't."

She backed off, her fierce expression growing milder. "All right," she said reluctantly. "But as soon as you get this ship checked out, you come to sickbay for five minutes. People need maintenance just as machines do. We can't afford to have you pass out at a crucial moment."

He started to tell her that he wouldn't, but another wave of dizziness warned him that she was right. She knew her job just as well as he knew his.

Sighing, he nodded, accepting the compromise. Beaulieu walked off the bridge, leaving him free to sag against the console.

It was already probably too late for Kelly and the others. Siggerson sighed again. They still had to go back.

8

Nash materialized in waist-deep water. Rain was falling in a heavy sheet, and at first he was completely disoriented. For one panicky second he thought he was drowning. He flailed and splashed frantically, then his knee bumped into a stump. He fell, going completely under. But his hands and knees hit shallow ground. He jerked to his feet and realized the water was only waist deep. Everything came back into perspective. He stood still, breathing raggedly, and looked around to get his bearings.

Fetid swamp enclosed him. He missed the pellucid light and cobalt sky of Zoe with a sudden fierce ache. Here, the sunlight was obscured by clouds. Towering trees blocked the sky. Their spreading branches reached low, snaking down almost to the muddy surface of the water. Moss hung upon the branches, making the trees look tattered. Knobby roots surfaced in clusters around each trunk like a defense zone. Rain streamed down trunks and off gigantic, fan-shaped leaves, caught in the moss and dripped from the ends, danced upon the water's surface, and drummed upon Nash's shoulders and back like a thousand stinging needles.

He was supposed to be half a kilometer from the

compound—but which way? He couldn't see anything, not even a spire of smoke, to give him a clue. Taking out a hand scanner from his pocket, he checked to make sure no water had gotten through its seal. He had taken it from the neat rack of scanners in the teleport bay. He wished, as he activated it and swung it around for a directional, that he'd had time to break into their armory for a weapon.

Those arrogant Hawks thought they knew god-all about deploying a rescue mission, but they'd made a mess of things. When he'd listened to their plans he knew they'd get Cassandra killed.

He'd taken them one by one as easily as though they'd been civilians. He'd nearly had their ship as well. As soon as he'd first seen it, he'd known it was the perfect bargaining chip, the one item of Alliance technology that no one in the Mechtaxlan Cartel could buy or steal. He had given Frant information on the Hawks and promised him the ship in exchange for Cassandra. And it was every bit of it worth her life.

Now, however, the Hawks had wrecked his plans. If he didn't hurry and try this last-ditch effort to rescue her, Frant would probably kill her.

Worry kept stitching its way through Nash's innards. He hadn't been able to think straight, to clear himself of this burning worry, ever since he first heard of Cassandra's abduction. She didn't know he was in love with her. He would never permit her to know. But he had sworn to serve her at any cost to himself or those around him. As soon as she left Zoe, however, he failed her. He, her trusted security adviser. What good had he been? He hadn't even been aboard the ship taking her to the Alliance Council, and he should have been despite her insistence that she didn't need him at her side.

Now he had to get her out. There could be no more failures, no more mistakes.

Pushing up his sleeve, he unclipped the small receiver which registered the signal from her transponder. Still receiving. It registered two other signals as well, but he tuned them out. Only Cassandra mattered. He wasn't interested in her staff. In the future, Cassandra's aides would be highly trained security personnel able to defend her from attack. Clerical skills could be handled by others. He would choose them himself.

By careful tuning, he was finally able to get his scanner on the same frequency as the receiver. The scanner alone could not register her transponder, but by using them in tandem he was able to isolate a direction.

He waded forward, pushing the water with his hands in a swinging motion. After a few minutes the water grew more shallow, receding to his knees, then his ankles. He splashed along quickly, hopping over the tangled footing of exposed roots. Tall mud spires that collapsed at the slightest touch stood along the bank like a miniature city. He toppled several of them, and beetle-looking creatures scuttled frantically. Small, stinging insects attacked him, drawing blood with innumerable, vicious bites that had him slapping and swearing. Something mournful called in the distance. The eerie sound of it sent prickles along his spine.

His right foot stepped in a bog hole and he plunged in up to his groin. The jolting wrench to his body stunned him for a moment, then he gathered his hands and his free left leg and pulled himself out of the clinging, sucking mud that tried hard to hold him prisoner.

A more savage cry rent the air, near enough to whip Nash's head around. Sweat poured into his eyes. Panting with fear, he found the super-human strength to pull harder. His leg came loose centimeters at a time, and he pulled until he felt his veins swell. His muscles burned with the effort. As last, with a horrid belching smack, the mud released his foot. He tumbled backwards and lay there unheeding in the swamp, relief sobbing in his throat.

He had lost his boot.

Swearing, he scrambled onto his all fours and plunged his hand into the bog hole. But it was useless. His fingers touched nothing, and he nearly trapped himself again.

It did not matter, he told himself, driving away despair so that he could keep functioning. He still had a job to do.

Smearing the sticky mud across the exposed areas of his face and neck, he gained himself some relief from the biting insects. Collecting the scanner from where he'd dropped it, he started on.

The ground was repulsively warm and fluid beneath his bare foot. Stobs from reeds torn off raggedly by some trampling creature cut and stabbed him. Soon he was limping. His speed was cut in half.

Time was running out. He quickened his pace, ignoring the pain.

The rain stopped abruptly, bringing on a sudden silence that was almost disorienting. Nash paused, panting. The heat was sapping him quickly.

In the distance he heard rhythmic sounds of chopping. He realized it must be the harvesters.

Anger clouded him. If Cassandra was out there, plastered with mud and leeching insects, her elegant hands blistered from manual labor . . .

He got a grip on himself. Frant had assured him Cassandra was being well-treated. He had to believe that. If he didn't stop letting his emotions get out of hand, he wouldn't be able to function.

A wild, mournful sobbing came from behind him. He glanced over his shoulder in spite of himself, but saw nothing. Shrugging, he trudged on. As long as it was daylight, he didn't expect to be attacked by any of the native wildlife.

He kept to the top of the bank, away from the shallow channel of water. Because his attention was focused on his scanner, he did not see the pair of luminous green eyes just above the surface of the water ten meters behind him. As he walked, making sure he did not cross paths with the harvesters or their guards, the eyes glided after him in silent patience.

In his office within the compound, Frant snapped the toggles in annoyance, trying to adjust the communications line that had vanished. At first he assumed it was mere interference. Sunspots, radiation from the defense moon, cross-line chatter from the other ships in orbit, any number of things. But static should have remained and the line should have cleared almost at once.

It did not.

"They aren't sending," said Elga.

Frant snorted and rose to his feet. As always, his movements were graceful, quick, and economical. He stood there a moment, severely annoyed and using that emotion to fuel his thought processes. He had been born a thinker—an exceptional, rare genetic spinoff of extremely high IQ and reasoning powers. A human computer, able, unlike the organic models developed by the Othians, to move and act and live. He was also a telepath—well, to be honest, a pre-telepath. That meant he could almost read other people's minds. It was like peering through a grubby window into a shadowy interior. He caught glimpses, as frustrating as they were tantalizing, and made do with guesses and his own analytical powers of deduction. He had gotten quite good at it over the years, good enough in fact to get away with calling himself a telepath. Mechtaxlan had never learned the difference.

"I don't like this," he said aloud. "Nash was cut off in mid-sentence. That means he does not have control of the ship. Instruct Defense to open fire."

Elga frowned. "You're going to destroy it?"

Frant considered the beautiful ship shimmering on the viewscreen. It was a marvel of Minzanese engineering. He supposed like all military vessels it had teleport capabilities. Mechtaxlan would be interested in having that technology, which was denied to civilians. But on the whole it was better not to have the ship as a distraction.

"Destroy it," he said.

Elga went on frowning, but she didn't argue further. She relayed the order. Frant stood by the viewscreen and watched the *Sabre* hold firm under the first barrage. Admiration tinged him.

"Excellent shields," he murmured.

The second barrage caused damage.

"One more is all it can take," said Elga. "Mr. Frant! It's moving."

"Of course."

He watched the ship roll in an incredible maneuver. Although he knew it was an illusion, the ship seemed to go from a standstill to time distort speed in seconds. She blurred and vanished, leaving only a light stream of distortion rippling in her wake.

"It's getting away!" said Elga. "The missiles—"

"Futile," said Frant. "The pilot will crash within the system. We'll send a salvage crew out later." He turned away from the viewscreen, dismissing the matter. Nash had been an interesting diversion, but Frant's orders were to keep Cassandra Caliban a prisoner until his superior Basft came in person to take her off Kenszana. He did not intend to deviate from those orders.

"Elga," he said, aware of the Boxcan's exasperation but

indifferent to it. "Have you the production reports? If that generator is still performing at half power, I want a replacement request sent off immediately."

"Yes, Mr. Frant," said Elga.

She handed him a list, and he scrolled the figures rapidly, able to read an entire page at a glance. He would have to make another tour of the production plant this afternoon. And fourteen workers were either dead or too seriously ill to continue working on the assembly. He considered the option of halting production for the five hours necessary to water down the inside of the plant. It was the only way to filter the rostma dust from the air. Breathing it all the time eventually caused major cell damage in the workers' brains. The poor fools usually died in blissful delirium, believing they were telepathic or else able to understand the mysteries of the cosmos. It was all a delusion caused by the systematic rupturing of cells within their pineal body. No drugs would ever give them what he had.

Or he could maintain current production levels and simply replace the workers with harvesters. He knew the value of proper plant maintenance, but next week they would be moving the compound and a shutdown would be mandatory then. He would replace the workers now and keep production going in the meantime.

Handing the list back to Elga, he said, "Inform Orson that I want fourteen replacements off the harvesters. Choose the weakest."

"Yes, Mr. Frant. Do you want the gangs renumbered, or do you want one gang smaller than the others?"

"Leave one smaller," he said. He disliked asymmetry. But this time for novelty's sake, he would operate one depleted gang until the compound move. Then everything could be reorganized at once.

A tap on the door made him frown. "Yes?" he said impatiently.

A technician stuck in his head. "Excuse me, Mr. Frant. Sensors are reporting a ship entering our space."

"Ah? Thank you."

The technician vanished and Frant raised his brows at Elga, who hastily routed the data to her station. The viewscreen activated to show them a few vague constellations shining against space.

"It's not in short scanner range yet," she said. "We should have visual in a few more minutes."

He knew that. He disliked having simple things explained to him. But Elga was peering at the viewscreen and did not see his frown. He considered whether it was time to replace her. His assistants never lasted long. He did not tolerate mistakes or patronization.

"It's probably the *Sabre* returning," he said, losing interest. "The Hawks are notorious for sticking to their job. And I'm sure they want to rescue Kelly. Perhaps we can have that ship yet. As soon as it's within range, instruct Defense not to fire on it."

"Yes, Mr. Frant."

"Notify me when it returns to orbit. I'll be touring the plant."

Picking up a filter mask, he left the office.

The approaching ship, however, was not the *Sabre*. As soon as it plunged out of time distort into normal speed, 41 jacked himself loose from his safety harness and began pacing across the cramped quarterdeck. The three other mercenaries present yawned and kept their seats, not even bothering to watch Kenszana looming ever closer upon the viewscreen. Below deck, bunked two to a cabin, the remaining force of ten probably were equally indifferent. They took their orders, went out and did their job, and came home to collect their pay. That's all it meant to them.

41, however, burned with anxiety. If the fool Kelly still lived. If he had come soon enough or too late. If this compound could be destroyed.

Normally he had the ability to detach himself from concern and emotion. He separated his actions from the core of what he was. In the past it had sometimes been the only way to survive. Now, when he needed that ability most of all, he remained clouded with emotions, all of them conflicting. They kept him on edge and barely in control when he needed a mind razor sharp in order to deceive Harva Opie's men.

He had sold himself back to Harva in order to save Kelly. It was not possible to tell Kelly that he had once been a harvester on Kenszana, sold to Frant like a piece of meat, subjected to brutality, and worked until he dropped. To make even one small admission was to open the gates and let all the bad memories out.

He had been smaller then, not full grown. He had learned to speak Glish on Kenszana. He had learned not to strike out in self-defense but to wait, enduring whatever was done to him, until the moment came for retaliation. He did not want to remember the electric prods jolting him until he thought his heart would stop and he would die there in the water and the mud. He did want to remember the coscacun—a large carnivorous reptile that swam beneath the water and clipped off the legs of harvesters too slow to flee. He did not want to remember the nights—when the air was so hot and thick that it smothered, and the strongest harvesters preyed on the weak. In the mornings the guards often found one or two dead. They always thought the workers had died of exhaustion; 41 knew better.

And what about the escape attempts? Workers either perished in the swamps as food for the coscacuns, or fell into bog holes and suffered there until the owts, who had dug them, returned to check their traps. If recaptured by guards, escapees had their hamstrings cut and thereafter dragged themselves about through the mud for the short remainder of their pitiable existence. Most of them committed suicide. It was easy enough to fall on a reed stob and let it pierce the jugular vein.

The stink of rostma hung over the refinery like a cloak. Inside, the air was so filled with dust the huge machinery and rows of workers operated in a perpetual haze. To breathe was to die, for the dust was addictive. Guards in filter masks routinely dragged out workers convulsing horribly as their few remaining brain cells exploded. They died, bleeding from the nostrils and ears, their eyes wide open in an ecstasy that was a lie. They never knew they were dying. Perhaps that was merciful.

Where was Kelly in all of this? He was a fool to go into it, a fool not to listen to warnings, a fool not to realize that the ambassador should be written off and all of Kenszana destroyed from space. It, and the other labor-intensive production planets, were like ulcerating sores on a plague victim. Kelly had seen much suffering and evil; it was why he made himself a Hawk, in order to fight such things. But Kelly had never really suffered himself, and because of that he could not truly understand when it was better to avoid a thing. He believed that his squad could deal with Kenszana as it had dealt with every other mission. Kelly was wrong not to realize that he had limits.

"We're in orbit," said Taft, the mercenary captain Harva had put in charge. "You ready, 41? Everyone, get geared up and pack the shuttle."

Grunting acknowledgment, the mercenaries left the quarter-deck. 41 stood alone with Taft and the pilot, who shut down her station and leaned back with a slo-stick in her mouth.

Taft already wore half of his armor, making his torso barrel-thick. He was as tall as 41, but twice the weight. Alone, he filled the cramped space of the quarterdeck. Unshaven, with a large emerald glittering in his ear and his small red eyes alight with the kind of controlled madness only true psychopaths have, he possessed cunning and shrewdness to go along with his size.

He had started working with Harva Opie, since 41's service, but plainly he was not to be tangled with. He glared at 41.

"You moving? You staying? You got anything else about this hit you want to share before we go down?"

41 met his stare. "Let's go."

He started off the quarterdeck, but Taft's hand seized him and slung him around. The pent-up fury in 41 sent him kicking out, aiming at a vulnerable spot beneath Taft's armor. He connected and heard Taft grunt, but then Taft retaliated with an augmented punch to 41's stomach. The extra muscle kick in the blow doubled 41. He wheezed for breath, all the strength leaking from his knees. His stomach felt like it had ruptured. He wanted to puke, but he hadn't enough breath.

When the yellow agony finally drained from his vision, he glanced up at Taft towering over him. Taft gripped him by the front of his jerkin and lifted him. Slammed against the wall, 41 winced and dropped his hands away from his gut. It still hurt, spasming with spirals of hot torment, but he wasn't seriously damaged. He met Taft's gaze, aware that Taft could have killed him with that single blow if he had wanted.

"You remember," said Taft. "You remember who you belong to now."

41 struggled to get enough breath to speak. "I have not forgotten."

The admission in itself was a surrender, as he had surrendered himself to Harva, as he would go on surrendering until his spirit broke, or they killed him. Shame flooded him, and he wanted to kill Taft, to fight him here and now until nothing remained of either of them.

But there was Kelly, who had to be saved. His friend, for whom he would let himself be destroyed. It did not seem fair, but it had to be done all the same.

Taft shoved him. "Move. Time to be going."

Kelly spent the rest of the day stacking the small, processed rostma bales on grav-flats. Each bale weighed about five kilos. That in itself was light, but the guards insisted he pick up an armload of bales each time. He had to juggle them, afraid of what contact of the dust on his bare skin might do, back and forth at a steady pace. If he dropped a bale, it was likely to spill from its packaging. That brought him a clubbing from the guard assigned to watch the loading. Periodically he was prodded. The jolt was painful and unnecessary since he was working as fast as he could. The guard seemed to derive great pleasure from shocking him. After a while, Kelly's arms and fingertips began to tingle constantly, not just whenever he was jolted.

His shoulders were not up to the work. Imperfectly healed and infected, they exploded with pain each time he picked up a load. He had to ignore it, however, and stagger on. The tapo patch had long since lost its effectiveness in blocking the pain. He felt drained and feverish, but at least he was outside and in a fairly central area of the compound where he could catch glimpses of Cassandra's quarters as he moved back and forth between the loading dock and the grav-flats. Why this wasn't done robotically, he did not know. Good automated equipment had to be a much cheaper investment than live workers.

A dull popping sound from overhead almost made him look up. He avoided that mistake and went on with his work, but inside he began to grin, feeling hope for the first time since Methanus. The popping sound came again. Several seconds later it came again.

"What the hell is that?" said the guard aloud, staring at the sky.

Kelly threw his armload of bales at the man, knocking him off balance just enough for Kelly to seize the prod from his hand. Kelly jolted him in the throat, and the guard went sprawling, unconscious or dead. Kelly did not bother to check.

A second guard was on the other side of the loaded grav-flats. He would stroll back in a minute. But a minute was all that Kelly needed.

Kneeling, Kelly swiftly took the first guard's scoped pistol, communicator, and force wall key that would enable its bearer to step through the shields encompassing the compound. He darted beneath the loading dock just as the second guard came into sight.

There was a shout. Kelly threw himself on his belly and squirmed farther in beneath the refinery crawlspace. He heard an alarm, and his own nerves jumped.

Calm down, he told himself. *Don't respond to the noise.*

Crawling on his belly put a fresh variation of strain on his shoulders. He grimaced and kept going, burrowing in like the mud beetles. It was not really a place to hide; he did not intend it as such.

There wouldn't be a single hiding place in this compound. It had too many sensors and security monitors. Escapes had been tried before; they could not have succeeded.

But Kelly wasn't after escape right now. Someone, presumably Phila, was deploying scatter charges into place for later detonation. Right now they must all be resting on the top barrier sealing the compound. Those popping noises came from the energy friction between the shield and the charges as they landed.

It felt unbelievably good to know that the *Sabre* had arrived and his backup team was in place. They weren't doing what he'd outlined for them, but right now that didn't matter. He meant to cause all the diversion and confusion he could.

He was well under the refinery now. He could hear and feel the throbbing rumbling of the machinery. It was very warm under here. Dark and damp as well. The mud smelled sour. He paused for a few seconds of rest, his own panting echoing in his ears. The moisture which had soaked through his clothes felt clammy against his feverish skin. He could feel his pulse throbbing in a band below his eyes, keeping time with the beat of the machinery. Insects crawled and scuttled over his hands, making him jerk in revulsion.

To distract himself, he thumbed on the communicator.

". . . and recall all harvester gangs," said Frant's precise voice. "Immediately."

Kelly frowned. He'd expected to hear orders to search and recapture him. So much for diversion and confusion.

Perhaps Frant wasn't searching for him at all. Perhaps Frant had simply slapped additional guards around Cassandra Caliban. If Kelly came out, he would be spotted. If he went outside the force wall, he could be tracked down or allowed to die in the swamp.

Annoyed, Kelly started crawling again. He didn't like Frant and his cold-blooded way of doing things. He would stir this place up no matter what it took, but first he had to get to the ambassador. Get her out of the quick-set and get her out of the compound.

Ahead of him, daylight bent a gray angle of illumination beneath the edge of the refinery. Kelly slowed down and thumbed on the communicator again. This time there was lots of chatter and commands being given. Most of it had to do with locations of the gangs, how close to quota they came today, and warnings to stay alert when the force wall was opened.

Snorting to himself, Kelly tried adjusting his communicator to a longer range. But all it did was squawk shrilly in his hand. He turned it off hurriedly and slithered close enough to the edge of the building to see out from beneath it.

Pairs of guards with weapons unslung and ready moved along purposefully, making quick scanner sweeps. He had crawled along to this side of the refinery to have a clear vision of the ambassador's quick-set. Sure enough, the guards had been doubled.

To get to the ambassador, he would have to cross at least fifty meters in the open. The guards would have clear sight of him all the way and could play target practice as much as they wanted.

Rolling onto his side, Kelly pulled out the weapon he had taken and examined it. Laser-scoped for accuracy, it was a well-balanced, waterproofed percussion pistol with dual action loading, which made it a few seconds faster between shots than the more conventional types of percussion weapons. In the hands of an amateur it would provide a fast stutter of bullets, but would run out of ammunition quickly. In the hands of an expert, it was deadly, accurate, and almost fast enough to compete with plasma weapons.

Kelly was an expert. He checked the action, checked the clip, which was full, and checked the scope. He curled his fingers around the butt and gripped hard, holding it until the scope's tiny computer chip registered his imprint. Now it would work in tandem with him, focusing on the involuntary pulse points in his palm and at the base of his fingers, linking through energy manifestations from the synapse clusters of his nerve endings and working that much better for him.

All the same, it wasn't much against four guards with rifles.

He surveyed the situation again. It didn't get any better. *When is Phila going to detonate those charges?* he wondered impatiently.

Not until I give her a signal.

He scuttled back under the refinery. Blowing it up should be signal enough. All he had to do was make sure he didn't blow himself up with it.

9

The generators were overhead, visible through the ventilation grille beneath them, and vibrating busily. By the time he
reached them, Kelly had nothing left. He told himself that was
just the down side of the drug, nothing more. He could get
through this. He didn't *need* any more tapo, dammit.

But as he lay there in the mud, fumbling to get his pistol up,
a sudden wave of weakness went through him, washing the last
of his energy away. His hands trembled, and he gripped the
pistol hard to keep from dropping it in the ooze, swearing
angrily again and again beneath his breath.

If he just had a little, he could go on. . . .

No!

Kelly forced it off and willed his hands to stop shaking. He
rolled onto his back and aimed his pistol at the small round
circuit-access box that was the generator's Achilles heel.
Before he could lose this instant of self-control, he fired.

A hissing sizzle preceded sparks that shot violently in all
directions. The steady throb of machinery faltered. A warning
rumble shook the generator, and in alarm Kelly flopped onto
his belly and started crawling away as fast as he could. It could
simply malfunction or it could blow sky high. If the latter
occurred, he didn't have a chance under here.

Nothing exploded. After several panicky seconds, Kelly slowed and forced himself to gulp in some deep breaths. His heart stopped pounding quite so hard.

Now for the backup generator.

But just then he heard the loud whoop of an alarm. To his right came a clanking rattle and a series of clicks. The building above him began to lower.

Fear kicked the back of Kelly's throat. Belly-flat, he crawled as fast as he could, aiming away from this central section of the modular unit and praying that it was the only part coming down as its grav supports shut off.

The alarm continued to whoop, escalating in volume with every passing second. Kelly realized that he had done more damage to the generator than he intended. It was going to blow, and lowering the units to the ground was a built-in safety feature to the whole system design to keep the units from tumbling in the blast.

He could see daylight ahead.

Move, Kelly. Move, move, move.

His breath was like a saw in this throat. His shoulders and arms were on fire. His body weighed tons and got heavier with every passing moment as more mud clung to him. He was bogging down in it. Soon he was going to be pressed flat, part of the ground, with all the juices crushed out of him.

The unit brushed his shoulders. The alarm deafened him. He tried to move faster, but he wasn't going to make it. He couldn't pull himself another centimeter. The unit was squashing him, holding him in place no matter how much he squirmed and kicked. Daylight was so close, so damned *close*. He was pinned now, wriggling furiously, still making a little progress, but not enough. His outstretched hand grasped the edge of the unit and clamped there desperately.

He twisted his forearm to get the right angle of leverage and pulled with all his might. Pulled until the tendons in his wrist strained and the cords stood out in his neck. Pulled until he was screaming with the effort.

And the mud had him, hanging on with just as much determination. Its softness gave beneath him, granting him a few more seconds of life from the unit coming down. He went on pulling, his legs scissor-kicking frantically.

His head was out. The low angle of daylight left was

disorientating. He saw crates and a stockpile of supplies swathed in waterproof sheeting. But all his mind could really register was the weight, settling in, unbelievably heavy. The mud beneath him bubbled with displaced water. He scooped it out from beneath his pelvis and gained enough space to drag himself out to his knees. He panted, digging his fingers into the ground, straining until his vision blurred and his blood roared in his ears.

His feet. They were snagged. Damned feet stuck on the end of his ankles like twin anchors. He twisted and struggled, beyond thinking now, knowing only the fear that was like a bitter, metallic tang in his mouth. He wasn't going to make it. He couldn't make it. He—

The final squelchy thud of the unit panicked him. He froze, his eyes clenched shut, unable to breathe as he waited for the agony to come rushing up his nerve endings to his brain. Nothing. His severed ankles remained numb. Maybe it was a mercy. But how long until he bled to death?

Determined to face it, he opened his eyes and looked. His feet were a good five centimeters clear of the unit. He'd made it.

Shocked, he stared for a moment. Then he sagged, hiccuping and choking in relief. Slowly he drew up his trembling legs and let the adrenaline shake through him.

"Warning. Personnel should evacuate. Warning. Personnel should evacuate."

The synthesized voice spoke calmly over the alarm. Kelly realized dimly that he should get moving.

He climbed to his feet like an old man. His sense of balance was gone. He swayed, staggered, and caught himself. Somehow he got his feet moving. Two steps, five, six. . . .

The blast caught him in an enormous roar that filled the world with heat and light so blinding that his senses could not register it. The concussion lifted him off his feet and tossed him like a helpless rag. He went pinwheeling through the air on a ride that seemed to last forever. Part of him enjoyed flying. The rest knew that when he ever came down it was going to be too hard. At least he had given Phila her signal. He wished, however, that he could have met Cassandra Caliban face to face just once.

He saw the ground come rushing up fast. He was surprised

at how fast, then it hit him so hard he cried out. He skidded and rolled over, crashing into something solid that made the world go out of focus. Stuff thudded down upon him.

Rostma dust, he thought wearily and then blacked out.

Caesar wasn't sure how he always drew water duty on their missions. The boss seemed to have an uncanny sense about sticking him wherever it was sure to be wet.

Hacking at iron-hard roots with a blunt machete, and trying to be sure he didn't cut off his own foot instead, was certainly the most interesting water-related experience he'd had yet. With most of the root knees underwater, every swing was a blind one. It was necessary to either lop off the top of the knee or to make a V cut from each side in order to get at the soft stringy insides that rostma eventually came from.

Even if he didn't cut off his own leg, he stood a good chance of grabbing a poisonous snoat or a baby coscacun or a real bad whatsit of some kind, instead of the rostma pulp. It had happened enough today to several other workers to make Caesar real nervous about plunging his hand down into the muddy water and groping around.

The damned pulp had to be kept wet or it lost its potency. Caesar got it into the air as often as he could, and every time he did a guard zapped him with a prod. He was beginning to feel pretty spazzed.

But at least he'd found Thessic Sazt—a queer, leathery little guy who was a Zoan aborigine. Caesar liked him on sight. He was as big around as a piece of fiber optic cable and about as tough. He knew what he was doing with a machete, not that the guards ever got close enough for him to try anything.

That was one aide found. The other one, Thessic had whispered hurriedly during their break, was dead. So Jon Porto could be crossed off the list of things to do. Caesar hacked, making more splash than actual work, and worried about how Kelly was doing. By now that cyborg Frant probably had Kelly's guts strung across the compound for a clothesline.

As for Janitte Krensky, Thessic had no idea of what had become of her. He hoped she was with the ambassador. Caesar, however, knew that only the ambassador had any hostage value and did not share Thessic's hope. He remembered what Janitte looked like from their briefings, and thought a torp casing would win a beauty contest before she did. He figured the poor woman was either dead by now like Porto, or in the refinery. Either way, she was dead.

He took a vicious swing at a large old root. The machete bounced off without making even a scratch. The jolt went right up Caesar's wrist.

"Damn!" he said aloud.

Too loud. One of the guards heard him and came floating over on his cute little gravity boots for another prod. But Caesar had had enough shocks. He forgot about not causing trouble and swung up his machete to parry the prod before it could touch him. Electricity sizzled in blue streaks along the machete blade. The hilt absorbed it, conducting it into Caesar's palm.

He cried out in pain, but his hand spasmed closed around the hilt and would not turn loose. The current felt like it was coming out the top of his head. His teeth clattered and he could feel his tongue trying to go down his throat.

Then the charge failed on the prod. The machete went spinning through the air and dropped into the water with a hiss of steam. Caesar's whole arm felt numb. He stood there, gagging and gasping, too stunned to think.

"That's it for you," said the guard angrily. He turned to another guard. "Give me your prod."

"Mr. Frant said no—"

"Give me your prod!"

With a shrug the second guard handed it over. By now the fuzzy mists around Caesar were clearing. He floundered back, losing his footing, and fell. The prod missed him.

Cursing, the guard came after him. Before he could attack Caesar again, however, a tremendous blast in the distance shook the swamp. Everyone turned to look. In the direction of the compound an orange fireball glowed briefly above the treetops.

Caesar didn't wait. He didn't speculate. He didn't stand there and stare with the others. A chance was a chance.

He gulped a breath and dropped into the waist-deep water, submerging before anyone realized what he was doing. The water was so muddy he couldn't see a thing, but he was betting on the guard not moving position. As soon as he thought he was under where the guard was hovering, Caesar shot up, using his palms to twist the guard off balance.

The contact between his skin and the bottom of the gravity boots brought instant, searing anguish. But the guard went crashing into the water, where his boots immediately shorted out. While he was floundering and cursing, Caesar yelled at Thessic and dived under the surface again.

He wanted to reach the deep part of the channel. There, he might have a chance at escape, although he couldn't hold his breath forever and he couldn't really swim in these shackles. Something whizzed past his elbow. Something else grazed his side. He realized he was being shot at and scrambled faster through the murky water, his lungs bursting for the breath he dared not surface for.

But as tricky as his situation was at the moment, he didn't really care. He was too busy gloating inside. Why had he ever worried about Kelly's little tapo addiction? Kelly was as tough as they came. From the looks of things, he'd managed to blow up the compound. And with nothing on him but one little molar cap bomb. Not bad.

Caesar tipped back his head and stuck the tip of his nose above water. Little plops ringed his head. More bullets. He managed to get air without sucking in a snout full of water and made the channel.

The ground dropped out from under him all too suddenly. The water temperature lowered a couple of degrees, and he felt the slight tug of a current. *Out here's where the coscacuns play,* he thought. They were about four meters long, all teeth and claws. He wished he hadn't thought about them.

He shot to the surface, bobbing awkwardly, and wondered how far the guards were going to let him get before they activated his shackles.

About then, he found out. The shackles on both his wrists and ankles fused, leaving him with his arms on the down-stroke. Unable to lift them, he floundered, sank, bobbed up and rolled onto his side as the current bore him along. He kept struggling against the shackles, desperate to at least move his arms so that he could keep his head above water, but they weren't budging. He gulped for air and got water instead. Choking, he rolled again so that his head was underwater. He struggled, trying to get onto his back, but he couldn't manage it.

In the distance he could hear the guards laughing. They weren't going to recover him or waste more ammunition on him. They were just going to let him drown out here and write him off as a cheap loss.

Infuriated, Caesar tried once more for air, got more water into his lungs, and started dying.

Crouched in the fork of a tree with her arm cradling the heavy, cylindrical bore of a launcher, Phila scanned the compound through her binocs once again. It was fully dark now, but she'd adjusted them to infrared. Since the refinery had blown, guards and workers were running about in every direction, but she couldn't spot Kelly or Caesar anywhere. Their transponder signals had been right together up till a few hours ago, then they'd separated. One went into the swamp; the other remained in the compound. That's when she, Siggerson, and Beaulieu came up with a change of plan. Kelly never liked to mount full assaults in hostage situations, but Phila figured they had to do something drastic this time.

The damage to the refinery wasn't total, despite the violence of the explosion. Only one of the three units had been destroyed. The fire had already been put out by the rain that was now falling in a steady downpour. Phila wiped her face and the back of her neck, being careful to avoid the sore spot on her skull. She hoped Nash was drowning somewhere, but she would rather carve her initials in his stupid, Zoan guts.

She flipped the setting on her binocs back to energy readouts. Multi-colored blobs and shifting patterns made her blink for a few seconds until her vision adjusted. The force wall wasn't powered directly by the damaged refinery generator, but power settings all over the compound were fluctuating erratically. The overhead seal was down and there were weak spots in the force wall. Her scatter charges were all in place on the ground now.

She shifted her position to keep her legs from cramping. She didn't want to detonate the charges until she had her people located.'

"See anything?" asked Beaulieu from the darkness below.

"Yeah. They're having power trouble. But there are too

many backup systems in this place. They'll be straightened out within an hour. We need to make our move *now* before we lose our advantage—"

"No," said Beaulieu impatiently. "Which one is in the compound? I mean, Kelly or Caesar?"

Phila lowered her binocs a moment in anger. "It shouldn't make any difference."

"Of course it makes a difference," retorted Beaulieu. "I'm betting Caesar is in the compound. He's reckless enough to start blowing things up on his own. And if he's there, then we can second-guess how he'll think and what he's likely to do next."

"Oh," said Phila. Her flash of temper faded quickly. She envied Beaulieu's ability to stick to a cool line of reasoning. "Caesar will hit the backup systems next. If he can get to them."

"I'm still reading the two Zoan signals in the compound. And one in the swamp near Kelly."

"Maybe Kelly."

"Don't quibble," snapped Beaulieu. "Oh, hell!"

The sudden despair in her voice made Phila glance down. "What is it? What's wrong? Antoinette?"

"I—I've lost our swamp signal," said Beaulieu in a choked voice.

Phila froze. She didn't want to think, didn't want to feel. "Zoan?"

Beaulieu didn't speak for several moments. By the time she answered, Phila knew the answer.

"No," said Beaulieu. "Ours. Damn. Oh, damn, damn, damn!"

"Calm down," said Phila, as much to herself as to Beaulieu. She didn't want to believe Kelly was dead. He was stern, sometimes stiff, and he put them through the toughest situations. But his blue eyes could suddenly soften with understanding. He never asked them to do anything he wouldn't do himself. He was the best commander she'd ever had. Without him, serving in the StarHawks just wouldn't be the same.

Phila's eyes filled with tears. She blinked hard. She remembered the training lectures on what to do if you lost a commander on a mission. Right now they were just words offering no comfort. Kelly *couldn't* be dead.

"Maybe the transponder is malfunctioning," she said.

"It can't," said Beaulieu shortly.

"Or your receiver has a glitch. Moisture inside the seal could—"

"*No*," said Beaulieu. "The only way for the transponder to fail is for the heart to stop. It runs off body energy. You know that."

"Yeah, I know," said Phila quietly. She trained her binocs back on the compound, but for a few moments she saw nothing through them.

"Now what do we do?" said Beaulieu.

"We finish," said Phila angrily. She slid her hand over the detonator switch, longing to press it. "We do our job. We wipe out these *scatsi*. We poison this swamp so no more rostma grows here. We *ruin* Kenszana."

"I don't think vendetta is part of our orders."

"It is now," said Phila.

"Phila, wait," said Beaulieu in alarm. "You can't start an assault until we—"

"You give me the bearings of those three signals within the compound," said Phila grimly, "and I'll set off charges accordingly."

"Phila—"

"Do it!" shouted Phila. "We've lost one. If we sit here on our butts, we'll lose more."

"And if the guards kill them as soon as we start an assault?"

That same thought had already occurred to Phila. She was afraid. Her hands weren't quite steady. And she was furious with Beaulieu for robbing her of the little confidence she had left. *What would Kelly do?* she asked herself. But she already knew the answer.

"We take the chance," she said. "Caesar is already mobile, or he wouldn't be blowing up chunks of the refinery. That means he has the best chance of rescuing the ambassador now. We have to support his actions. Get ready. As soon as I start detonating the charges, we've got to change our position."

Beaulieu didn't immediately answer. Phila frowned at the darkness, wondering if the doctor was going to accept her decisions. After all, the doctor outranked her and was about twice her age. It was hard to snap off orders to someone like that. And if Beaulieu refused to let her take charge? If Beaulieu kept arguing?

"I'm ready," said Beaulieu with a grunt, as though she'd just picked up the rest of the equipment. "Just remember that Siggeron's out of reach for the next four hours. Don't get us into too much trouble."

Phila nodded in relief. "Right," she said, and pressed the detonator.

10

A blast ripple woke Kelly. Groggily he opened his eyes. The world was red.

Frowning, he blinked and lifted his head. In the darkness fires were burning and a rapid-fire series of small blasts from the scatter charges went off every few minutes, throwing the compound into fresh confusion. Guards were running everywhere, trying to restrain workers or put out fires. The barracks were a smoking ruin. Kelly saw Frant himself, silhouetted against the fire, gesturing and shouting orders.

Instinctively Kelly drew himself up onto his hands and knees and scuttled for cover. He'd been thrown a long ways from the refinery. He was amazed to find himself still alive and relatively intact. His left leg wasn't working too well. Sharp pain shot through it when he put his weight on it, but it wasn't broken. He could walk on it. There was blood on his face and several other places. His ears still rang, but he wasn't seeing double. He was fine.

But he'd lost his gun. He had to get a replacement and keep the ambassador from getting blown up by Phila's scatter charges.

He set off at a low run, hobbling badly, but covering the

distance. In the general confusion no one was paying attention to him, but he kept to as much cover as he could find.

Within minutes he had stumbled over a man lying on the ground. He knelt swiftly and searched him for a weapon. Someone had beaten him to it. Disappointed, he scrambled to his feet and went on.

He had to make a lot of detours and dive for cover to keep out of the way of goon squads rounding up the screaming workers. Some threw themselves at the force wall. One got through, although it left him writhing in agony. He picked himself up and ran into the jungle. The others bounced off, yelling curses. Kelly grinned to himself. If the shields were weak, Frant's attention was going to be focused on having them restored as soon as possible, or he would lose his entire work force.

Kelly came across another dead guard. Again, no weapons. Exasperated, he looked for a live one off to himself, but they all seemed to be in pairs or squads. He gave up the idea and kept going toward the quick-set. The ambassador's guards were still in place, and the fire was heading in the other direction. So Cassandra wasn't in any immediate danger of being crisped in her quarters.

He still had to find a way to get her out. In desperation he hid himself behind one of the tow tractors and waited for a squad to trot by. He hurled himself out at the last man and tackled him sloppily from behind. It was more than reckless. All the guard's companions had to do was glance back and Kelly would be finished. But no one noticed.

The guard beneath Kelly was a tough one. He squirmed in mid-air, making sure he hit the ground on his side instead of face down. He rolled beneath Kelly, despite Kelly's efforts to pin him, and got a deathgrip on Kelly's throat.

At once his air cut off. Kelly instinctively reached for the guard's hands in an effort to pry them loose. But the guard only tightened his grip. Kelly's vision darkened. His lungs jerked in the need for air. The top of his head felt numb. He could hear his ears roaring. Not much time left.

While he still had strength, he had to retaliate. He gathered the remainder of his concentration and chopped his opponent in the throat with all the strength he possessed. The pressure on his own windpipe slackened. Kelly dragged in a mangled breath and struck the guard again, using the angle 41 had taught him, which snapped the man's neck.

Feeling faintly sick, Kelly rolled off his opponent and gulped in air until his head stopped buzzing. Then he seized the guard's rifle and picked himself up.

Almost at once, however, he paused. Slinging the rifle over his shoulder, he grabbed the guard's foot and dragged him into cover. Minutes later, he stepped out boldly in the guard's clothes with his rifle cradled over his right forearm. In this melee it was unlikely anyone would recognize his face. As long as he acted with authority, it would be given to him.

Accordingly, he walked across the open space to Cassandra's quick-set at as fast a pace as he could maintain without limping. Under his left arm he carried a charred rostma bale swathed in a piece of waterproof sheeting.

The four guards on duty had their weapons primed and ready. Kelly walked right up to the door.

"Frant sent me over here with this," he said. "It's for her."

One of the guards scowled at him, and Kelly knew an awful qualm. He'd made a mistake. What?

"That's Mr. Frant to you, same as to everyone else," said the man. "You new here, or what?"

Kelly looked down, mentally kicking himself. "Yeah," he said. "I keep forgetting."

"The hell you do," said the man. He looked more closely at Kelly, his eyes narrow with suspicion. "We haven't had any reinforcements in four months."

Tension knotted in Kelly's stomach. He tossed the rostma bale at the guard to the far left, shot the man who had challenged him, and swung his rifle butt at the next one.

The man crumpled, clutching his groin. The guard who ducked the thrown bale fired at Kelly, but missed in his haste. Kelly shot him, aware that he couldn't possibly turn back around fast enough to escape being gunned down by the last man. But the shot he expected never came.

As he turned, he saw the last guard crumple beneath a blow to the back of his head. A woman stood over him, her hair streaming wild over her shoulders, a connector wrench in her hands.

Kelly stared in astonishment. How had she gotten out here? She had to be . . .

"Ambassador Caliban?" he said.

She looked at him for a long, measuring moment. Then she whirled and ran.

He remembered belatedly that he was in the uniform of the enemy. He sprinted after her, his leg aching with pain. She might be a diplomat, but she could run like a gazelle. She outdistanced him, gaining with every stride. Kelly struggled to kick up his pace, feeling like a fool. Some rescue this was turning out to be.

He was tempted to shout after her, but he didn't want to give her away.

Still, he was losing her as his leg began to give out. Every stride felt as though a white-hot brand was shoved into his knee.

Another burst of scatter charges went off right in front of Cassandra. She screamed and tried to dodge, lost her footing in the mud, and went down. Kelly's heart jumped to his throat. He kept running, although every step wrenched a grunt from him.

He fell rather than knelt beside her, unable to see more than the shadowy outline of her in the darkness. "Ambassador? Cassandra?" he said urgently. "My God, if Phila's hurt you, I'll make cat meat out of her."

The ambassador gasped out a little moan, from pain or fear he couldn't tell. He gripped her arm, holding her in place.

"It's all right," he said. "I'm Commander Kelly of Allied Intelligence Special Operations. We're here to get you out."

She sat up and her long hair spilled like silk over his hand. "I don't believe you," she said. "You're wearing a Mechtaxlan uniform."

"It's a disguise."

"Maybe," she said. Her voice, although frightened, remained incisive. This was not a woman who let fear overwhelm her. "You could be lying to me, saying you're a rescuer, when in reality you're just trying to recapture me."

Kelly had the feeling of a man trying to save a drowning swimmer, only to be fended off. Her reasoning was logical. He knew he had to come up with a way to convince her quickly, before their hiding place was discovered. There was so little time, and he was very tired.

He pressed the small box into her hand.

She took it unwillingly. "What is this?"

"A key to get through the force wall. It's the only proof of my intentions that I can offer you right now. We don't carry identification while undercover. Besides, you saw me take down three of your guards. If you hadn't believed in me on some level, you wouldn't have saved my life."

"I wasn't saving your life," she said fiercely. "I was attacking my enemy. But this key . . ."

"You must trust me," he said. "There aren't many of us because we were afraid a large assault would get you killed. But Nash—"

"Colonel Nash?" she said quickly. "He's with you?"

"On the ship. Or he may be helping the operatives with artillery. Now do you believe me?"

She stared at him as though trying to judge him through the darkness. "Yes, I believe you."

"Good. Then let's get you out of here."

He started to climb to his feet as he spoke, but Cassandra laid a hand on his arm.

"No," she said. "My staff is here. Janitte Krensky, my secretary, and two aides—"

"I know their names," said Kelly. "Look, Ambassador. Forgive me for being blunt, but right now your life is more important than theirs."

She jerked away from him. "No! I won't accept that. We believe in equality on Zoe, Commander. I may hold a high office, but I am not irreplaceable. Besides, I am responsible for them. Surely you can understand that."

He did, perfectly. And his sympathy for her position did not make it any easier to convince her. The adrenaline that had been carrying him since he woke up from the blast had run down, leaving him spent. But if he let himself think about how tired he was, then he thought about that other need raging through his veins, burning him up, sucking all the juices from his tissues. He thought about abandoning this woman and breaking into Frant's quarters. There would be a supply there. One more hit and he could finish this mission . . .

With effort he squelched the temptation.

"I understand you," he said and his voice dragged with fatigue. "But your theories of equality apply to Zoe, not this place. You're naive if you think Zoe isn't threatening war right now to get you back—"

"They are so foolish! They leave themselves wide open for more incidents of this kind."

"I'll find Janitte Krensky if I can," said Kelly. "Your aides are on the labor gangs, and my man there is looking for them. We won't abandon anyone, but you must go to—"

She looked past him with a little gasp. His instincts warning him too late of trouble, Kelly turned.

Frant and four of his men stood there, silhouetted against the fires. Frant's pale hair gleamed in the weird light. Flames reflected and danced in his pupils. His coveralls were streaked with mud and ashes.

Kelly had the sensation of floating. Frant and his goons didn't even look real. If he closed his eyes they would go away. The whole world would go away, and all his problems with it.

No.

He gripped reality and clung to it. Hiding his pistol behind his leg, he stepped up even with Cassandra who was standing frozen.

"Well, Kelly, you have been very busy," said Frant. "Put down your weapons."

Kelly shrugged his rifle off his shoulder and let it fall.

"All your weapons."

The guards moved in closer. Reluctantly Kelly tossed his pistol away.

"Hand over the force wall key and communicator."

Kelly complied, hoping Cassandra had enough sense to keep her key hidden.

Frant glanced at Cassandra. "It is foolish to be out here, Ambassador. You could be injured."

"You didn't expect me to sit tamely in confinement when I had the chance to escape, did you?" she said, using scorn to seem unafraid.

"I underestimated you. I shan't do so again." Frant gestured to one of the guards, who stepped forward. "She is to be transported to my scoutship immediately. Find Elga and tell her to request the shuttle."

"Yes, Mr. Frant." The guard trotted away.

Frant's eyes glowed a dark maroon in the firelight. Meeting them, Kelly shivered involuntarily. He tried to consider how best to keep them from taking Cassandra into space. She'd be almost impossible to snatch off a ship. But if he could get word to Siggerson . . .

"As for you, Kelly," said Frant. "You must be tweaking by now. You can't go on nerves and adrenaline forever. How about a fresh patch?"

As he spoke he pulled a patch from his pocket and held it up.

Kelly stared at it, and the scant strength left in him drained away. It would be so easy to accept it. He could get Cassandra out, he would be able to think clearly again, and he would have his energy back. Wasn't that worth whatever it cost him in the long run?

"Take it," said Frant gently, holding it out to him. "I don't believe in denying a need. And you do need it, don't you, Kelly?"

Cassandra stepped away from Kelly. "You're an addict?" she said in disbelief. "And in Special Operations? How—"

"She doesn't understand, does she, Kelly?" said Frant, his voice soft, enticing. "Doesn't understand the sweet comfort that will take the pain away. You're tired, aren't you, Kelly? This will help."

Kelly's mouth was dry. His eyes were burning. All the veins in his body were burning. He *did* want it. Just one last time, he told himself. Beaulieu could always dry him out if he survived this. If he didn't survive, the tapo wouldn't matter. His hand shook as he reached out.

Frant dropped the patch in his palm with a smile that became a low chuckle.

The last bits of Kelly's self-respect responded to that laugh. Furious, Kelly threw the patch away and glared at him in fury. "You b-bastard." His voice shook; his whole body shook. Humiliation was raw within him. He wanted to kill Frant.

"It wasn't poisoned, Kelly."

For an instant Kelly wanted to go scrabbling through the mud, searching for it. But Cassandra was watching, her face perplexed, worried, and slightly repulsed. Kelly felt on fire with shame because she had seen this in him. He wanted to impress her and show her the best of what he could do, but instead, here he was groveling like some pathetic junk-head.

"Was it from your own private stash, Frant?" he asked.

Frant stiffened.

"Tapo was designed for cyborgs and people over-augmented. After all, there's only so much metal and bio-ware implants the body can stand. Then it goes into rejection. But tapo takes care of that, keeps the body from knowing what's been done to it. Keeps *you* alive, doesn't it, Frant?"

"That's Mr. Frant to you," said one of the guards.

"Shut up!" snapped Frant.

"You're a 'borg, Frant. Maybe the only thing human left to you is your skin. Is that why the cartel stuck you way out here on the backside of the galaxy? All of your talents and abilities are wasted here on this mudball. They ought to have you out on the front lines, dealing and running important ends of the organization. That's where you belong, isn't it, Frant? Only you're a 'borg, and 'borgs are something nasty, something less than human, something to be used but despised—"

Frant swung at him. It was an augmented punch, intended to kill. Kelly meant to duck, but his reflexes were slow. Before he could move, Cassandra stepped between him and Frant.

"Stop it, you barbarian—"

Her cry ended as Frant connected, striking her on the forehead instead of Kelly's throat. She crumpled at Kelly's feet, unconscious before she hit the ground. Horrified, Kelly knelt over her.

"Cassandra! My God—"

Rough hands dragged him back. Frant knelt over Cassandra and checked her pulse.

"You!" he snapped at one of the guards. "Pick her up. Gently! Get her to shelter and find Elga. Hurry!"

The guard picked up Cassandra and carried her away. Her head dangled over his arm. Her long hair, bedraggled and wet, was stained with blood. Kelly watched, hardly able to breathe. The remaining two guards flanked him, activating his fusion shackles so that he couldn't move his arms. He glared at Frant, who was staring after her.

"If she dies—"

Frant whirled on him. "If she dies, you'll be blamed for it. You'd better make certain she doesn't die."

"Me? How?"

Frant gripped his arm, nearly squeezing it in half. He had lost his composure. His eyes were wild. "You Hawks always carry a medic in your squads. I know that. You have one nearby now. On your ship perhaps. Get that medic here."

"I don't have a communicator."

"That will be supplied."

"What about your own medic?" asked Kelly although he was already thinking about how Beaulieu could be contacted.

"He died in the first explosion. You blew up the infirmary, which was located on one end of the refinery. As I said, Kelly, if she dies it will be your fault."

"The cartel will have you executed for incompetence, won't it?"

Frant glared at him. "You'll go to hell with me. I promise you that. Guards! Get him secured and tell Elga to make contact with his ship. Hurry!"

Dull thuds. A voice mumbling. Soft, gagging cries of misery.

Caesar didn't want to wake up. It was far more comfortable to be dead.

After a while he realized the cries belonged to him. Someone was slamming him, forcing water out of his lungs. He felt so bad he knew he had to be alive. His eyes fluttered open.

In the muted but clear light of a porta-lamp, unfamiliar faces ringed him. Branded, scarred, savage faces. Huge, blocky bodies encased in armor. Caesar blinked at them without comprehension. Where the hell was he?

One of the faces glanced away and yelled something that Caesar couldn't understand. It was a harsh, gutteral, abbreviated language that sounded like some kind of battle code. Caesar frowned. He started to say something, but he hurt too much. Breathing hurt. His stomach hurt. He felt that if he opened his mouth he would be sick again.

Someone came, shoving his way into the circle. Caesar stared up into those alien yellow eyes, that narrow face that he'd figured he'd seen for the last time back before Methanus.

"41," he gasped. "Yusus. What are you—"

41 gripped him by the shoulders and hauled him up to a sitting position. Everything spun around Caesar. He gagged wretchedly, but his stomach was empty. They had removed his fusion shackles, and he was grateful for that.

41 shook him. "We dragged you from the swamp. Where is Kelly?"

Caesar had to fight off another bout of dizziness. He wished

41 would stop shaking him. "Found Thessic Sazt," he said. "Made a break for it. Did he drown too?"

"No. He is alive. I have no use for him. Where is Kelly?"

Caesar smiled in relief. "Should have known you weren't really mad at him. 41 to the rescue, huh?"

Another man, bigger than the rest, with weird red eyes and a jaw like a ship's stern, joined the group. He snarled something at 41, who replied in the same language.

41 turned back to Caesar with a frown. "You are wasting time. Much is happening to the compound. Where is Kelly? With the harvesters or in the compound? Tell me quickly!"

"He's in the compound. Frant got suspicious of him as soon as we landed. Who are these guys? Friends of yours? They look like a pack of yo-yo mercs to me."

"Watch what you say. They know Glish." 41 stared at him a moment longer, as though he wanted to tell Caesar something, then he got to his feet.

Caesar scrambled up weakly. "Hey! Wait a minute. What about—"

But 41 walked away without glancing back. Puzzled, Caesar frowned after him. Something very peculiar was going on. 41 was always weird, but he usually wasn't this weird. And these mercenaries looked like a very rough bunch. The big one with red eyes stared at Caesar with a nasty smile that gave Caesar the willies. He stared back, trying to look impervious in the best Hawk manner, but Redeye only smiled more broadly. He drew his pistol on Caesar and aimed it right between Caesar's eyes.

"Bang," he said in Glish and laughed.

The others laughed too, and Caesar's mouth went so dry he couldn't believe he'd been drowning just a short while ago. He decided maybe it was better not to look this bunch in the eye too much. They were crazies all right, real loup-loodlers. One of them shoved him, and he stumbled along willingly to join Thessic, sitting on the muddy ground like something the fishes refused to eat.

"I have gladness you are alive, Caesar," Thessic whispered.

"Yeah, likewise," muttered Caesar, helping him to his feet. They fell into step because the crazies were breaking camp and motioning for them to get moving at the rear of the column. "What's that old saying? Out of the pan into the fire?"

"I do not have understanding of this saying," said Thessic. "It makes not much sense to me. Perhaps my Glish is imperfect as to this specialized collequialism?"

"Yeah," said Caesar with a sigh. His gaze roamed, counting thirteen of them clumping along with enough armor and equipment to take on an entire army. And up near the front was 41, not in armor, armed with only the weapons he had taken off the *Sabre*. His arms were streaked with bloodstains from leech bites. He definitely didn't look like he was in charge. 41 was always one step off the bridge at the best of times, but what the hell was he up to now?

Caesar had the depressing feeling that he was going to find out very soon.

11

Dodging through dark jungle with infrared goggles strapped on over her eyes, and weighted down with scanners, die-hard, and strings of ammo clips, Beaulieu sucked at the salt tablet under her tongue and wondered how much longer she could keep running after Phila. Her foot caught on a root, and she nearly tripped. Catching her balance, she came to a halt and leaned against a tree, panting heavily. Sweat was running off her in rivers.

"Wait," she gasped, gulping in air. Around her lay the warm stench of decay, plant life gone rampant, and the drifting smoke from the compound. "Phila!"

Ahead, Phila plunged to a halt and turned around. "We can't stop here. We must keep going. They're bound to be scanning beyond the force wall now, looking for us. We can't afford to let them pinpoint us."

Beaulieu didn't know how the petite Phila managed to jog along with that heavy launcher on her shoulder, but she knew she couldn't keep going like this.

"I have to rest," she said, still breathing hard. "I'm sorry. This humidity is deadly."

"I grew up in soup like this," said Phila. "At least walk."

"All right." Slowly Beaulieu pushed herself away from the support of the tree. She couldn't help but resent the easy stamina of Phila's youth. She hated growing old.

Her wrist comm beeped. Startled, Beaulieu brought it up and slapped off the signal quickly. "Beaulieu here," she said, ducking beneath a loop of vines hanging between two trees. "You're back early, Siggerson."

"Beaulieu, this is Kelly. Where—"

She stopped dead in her tracks. Astonishment mingled with relief filled her. At the same time she realized it must have been Caesar who had died, yet right now she was too relieved to grieve for him. "Kelly!" she said so loudly Phila turned and ran back to join her. "You're alive. What is—"

Phila gripped her arm. "Wait! How did he get a communicator? He went in without equipment."

"Don't be an idiot," said Beaulieu. "He has acquired one somewhere in the compound. Stand by, Commander. We're receiving you."

Phila pulled at her. "Keep moving! This is a trick."

Beaulieu moved reluctantly. "Commander, what are your orders?"

"Doctor, break that signal!" said Phila. "They're using it to lock onto us."

Beaulieu shoved free of her. "Shut up! Sorry, Commander. I'm listening."

"Beaulieu, I need you here right away," said Kelly.

There was something odd about his voice. It was flat and rather lifeless, not at all like his usual crisp, decisive tones. He was also vague, and that wasn't like him.

"Where, Kelly?"

Before he could answer, Phila tackled Beaulieu, knocking her to the ground. Stunned, Beaulieu lay there for an instant until she realized that Phila was attempting to wrench off her wristband. Beaulieu caught Phila by the chin and shoved her away, kicking her where it hurt. Phila grunted with pain and huddled up long enough for Beaulieu to scramble to her feet and draw her pistol. She had it aimed by the time Phila made it up.

"I'm taking the risk, Mohatsa," she said angrily.

"You'll get us killed. It's a trick, I tell you. That doesn't even sound like Kelly."

"Then split off," said Beaulieu. She unslung her scanner and the ammo string and tossed them at Phila. "Go!"

"*Kost ta houd mandale che krihatsa*!" said Phila in a fury. She picked up the scanner and ammo. "You're a fool. As good as dead."

"Safe flight," said Beaulieu ironically.

Phila snorted and ran off into the night. Letting out her breath, Beaulieu holstered her pistol and reactivated her comm, praying Kelly was still on the other end.

"Commander? Come in, please. Command—"

"—not much time," said Kelly. "Need you here. Ambassador Caliban is injured. Sorry."

Beaulieu started walking. She frowned, trying to judge rationally instead of with the kind of gut instinct that had panicked Mohatsa. "You don't sound so good yourself, Commander. What's wrong?"

"Frant has us in the compound. Escape attempt . . . failed. His medic . . . dead. Ambassador is seriously hurt. Dying. I . . . can't order you."

"Never mind that," said Beaulieu. "What is the nature and extent of her injuries? I have only a limited medikit with me, and my sickbay is . . . unavailable at this time. Kelly? Commander, are you there?"

"I am Mr. Frant," said an unfamiliar voice over the comm line. "Our scanners have located you approximately ninety-two meters from the east side of our perimeter. Please approach the force wall. Someone will be there to let you through."

"Who the hell asked you?" said Beaulieu in alarm. "Put Kelly back on."

"Kelly is no longer conscious. We do not need him. But we do need you. The ambassador must not die, Dr. Beaulieu."

She came to a halt, her heart hammering painfully. Phila had been right. It was a trap. One she'd fallen right into. But she was a doctor before she was an operative. Whether the ambassador needed medical care or not, Kelly certainly did.

"Why should I surrender myself to you?" she said.

"You are making stupid delays. You know the value of the ambassador's life as much as I do. If you refuse this errand of mercy, Dr. Beaulieu, how will you explain your actions to your superiors and to the government of Zoe?"

She scowled. Damn the man. He'd hit the crux of the matter.

There had to be some way to get in there without becoming another hostage, but she didn't know what it was. In the meantime, she was possibly jeopardizing lives with her own dithering and cowardice.

"Very well. Just make sure your sentries don't get trigger-happy and forget what I'm coming for," she said and broke the connection before she could back out.

Stripping off her goggles, she reset their compass direction so that the digital readouts on the goggles would keep her on course. Then she drew a deep breath and headed for the force wall.

The taste of sludge lingered on in Caesar's mouth. He kept swallowing and spitting, but nothing helped. Thessic was limping, and Caesar himself felt so stiff with weariness that he found it difficult to keep up. The mercs were carrying about seventy-five kilos of armor and weaponry apiece, sure, but they probably had little anti-grav packs strapped on to balance the weight, and they hadn't spent the day swinging a machete. Caesar's back was killing him, and they never rested.

Then the column came to an abrupt halt. Caesar nearly fell over Thessic in the dark. They stood huddled together. A couple of mercs faded off into the jungle. The others shone a muted torch over the ground.

Curious, Caesar elbowed his way through to see what they were looking at. When he saw the half-eaten corpse, he wished he hadn't.

It took all his willpower not to bolt entirely. 41 crouched by the remains and gingerly lifted a scrap of olive-colored cloth. He glanced at Caesar, who remembered he was a Hawk and better than the rest of these unwashed bilge-breathers. Caesar went forward to join 41 and even managed to look at the corpse.

He'd seen death in many forms for years. But it was one thing to see a slagged body and another to see one that had been chewed. Caesar swallowed, feeling clammy and unwell.

"It's Nash," he said in answer to 41's unspoken question. "The only Zoan uniform in this neck of the woods."

"How did he get down here?" asked 41. "He wasn't supposed to be part of the ground mission. Did Siggerson change his mind?"

"How should I know?" said Caesar. "I left the ship before you did, remember? And speaking of that, what are you doing? Who are these hulks you've scraped up? You let Kelly down, you know that? You hurt him. He thought he could count on you."

41's face was a wall. "I am here. Be silent," he said. "We have come to get Kelly out."

"And me?" said Caesar, piqued. "What about me?"

"You are rescued."

"Oh, yeah? I don't feel like it. I feel like a prisoner. And you don't exactly look in charge around here."

"It does not matter."

41 was always pretty tight-lipped, but Caesar had been through enough missions with him by now to tell when 41 was pulling a flake.

"Look, pal. You can be the inscrutable savage all you want, but in the meantime we've got a mission going steadily to pieces. We'd better start working together, or none of us are going to get out of this, least of all Kelly."

41 sighed. He tossed away the bloody scrap of cloth and wiped his hands. "We know there has been trouble in the compound. Kelly's planned assault has already started."

"Planned . . . uh, right," muttered Caesar.

"We will take the compound in the next half hour. We will remove Kelly and . . . others of value. Then it will be destroyed. No more rostma will be harvested on Kenszana."

Caesar snorted. "Yeah. Good intention. But even if you wipe the compound, Mechtaxlan will install another one in a few months. And don't tell me you're going to crack this mudball open from out in space, because I don't believe you have a battlecruiser with you."

"No battlecruiser," said 41. "But a way to make the trees die." Baring his teeth in the rather unpleasant grimace he considered a smile, he drew out a vial from his pocket. "Biological poison, designed to attack only rostma sources. Very little else will be disturbed. Maybe a few coscacuns will die." He nudged Nash's corpse with his toe. "Maybe not. I have poured seven of these vials into the water since we landed. I have more. Rostma does not grow everywhere on this planet, only in this specific region of the continent. The poison is not biodegradable. It will remain in the water table and gradually spread. The rostma trees will die, and they will not grow back."

"Well, okay," said Caesar, impressed in spite of himself. "You've been a busy boy. Now for the assault itself. I can help. Beaulieu fitted me with some special molar caps before I left. Small, contained blasts with good compression. Limited damage but useful."

For a moment 41's eyes softened. He looked genuinely amused. "You have explosives in your teeth?"

"Yo. I mean, there's only one other place I could carry them and some things I won't do even for the service," said Caesar with dignity. "I figure Phila used enough scatter charges to make mush of the place, but she had to be doing it pretty randomly with the launcher. It will lay down a fair placement, but not as good as if it's done with the short cannon. So there're bound to be a few things still standing. I can help."

"You are saying many words to convince me to give you a weapon," said 41. "It won't work."

"Damn you!" said Caesar in outrage. "Why am I a prisoner? Kelly hurt your pride a little, that's all. What are you planning on doing, grabbing him out of here and selling him somewhere to get back at him?"

Anger flared in 41's eyes, but all he said was, "You are a fool."

He rose to his feet, but Caesar slapped a hand on his chest to keep him from walking away.

"No, you don't," said Caesar. "You're either running this show or you've sold out. Which is it?"

41 looked away. "You know already. I will not play this human game of confession."

"41, *why*?" Caesar whispered in hurt. "We took you in. Made you a part of us. Wasn't that—"

41's mouth tightened. He pulled Caesar's hand from his jerkin and walked away.

Feeling as though he'd just swallowed a wasp, Caesar watched him. Thessic came up, his obsidian eyes swallowing the light without reflection.

"I thought you said this man was a friend," said Thessic softly.

"Huh?" Caesar shook himself out of his dark thoughts. "No. I never said that. You can't reform a savage, Thessic. You can wash him and put him in good clothes and give him a decent salary. But sooner or later he turns back to his true nature and stabs you in the back."

Thessic snorted. "Ten months ago on Zoe, a man in high government position made an anti-aborigine speech employing your argument. There exists a great schism on this issue. I have been called a savage because my skin is dark, I have fangs, and I hiss when I speak. But I do not think I have ever stabbed anyone in the back."

Consternation went through Caesar. "Hey," he said. "I didn't mean you—"

"No, but if you wish to insult this one who was your friend, find another reason to justify it."

Before Caesar could respond to that, the two mercenaries who had left returned, and they brought with them a small, muddy, struggling prisoner. Caesar stared, then hurried forward.

"Phila!" he said in excitement. "Hey, you overgrown brawnoids, turn her loose. Turn her loose!"

They had her by the arms. She was kicking and struggling so hard that her feet were off the ground. Her face glowed red with anger, and she was spitting curses both in Glish and her native language.

"41, for God's sake, tell your goons to turn her loose," said Caesar.

41 ignored him. It was Taft, the overgrown merc leader, who spoke the command. Phila was dumped onto the ground. At once she scrambled upright and came running to Caesar.

"Who are these *scatsi*?" she demanded breathlessly. Her black eyes were snapping. "What's 41 doing here? He's on the wanted list."

"Wanted list?" said Caesar stupidly. "What—"

"He jumped ship without security blocks."

Caesar blinked. "The hell he did. So that's why he's acting so unfriendly. Sold us out to his old mercenary pals."

Phila wiped her face. "They took the launcher and all the ammo. Not that there's much left, but—" Breaking off, she turned and stared at him as though she had never seen him before.

"What's with the look?" said Caesar.

"You're not dead."

Worried, he gave her a little pat on the shoulder. "Hey, toots, lighten that look. Maybe those bilge-breathers rattled your pan a little too hard. Why would I be dead?"

"We had your transponder signals on the scanner. Yours stopped sending, and the only way those things can fail is if your heart and lung activity stops."

Caesar frowned. He didn't want to think about how close he had come to drowning just a short time ago. Even now, he still felt wrung out.

"Just held my breath under water a while," he said. "Had to break out of the chain gang. Now I've hooked up with these guys. 41 says they're planning an assault on the compound. He plans to wipe it clean."

Phila's eyes widened. "You can't! I mean, they can't do that! Kelly's still in there. So's the ambassador and Beaulieu."

Before he could ask what the devil the doctor was doing there, Phila turned away and headed toward 41.

"Phila, come back!" said Caesar, but she ignored him.

Cursing, Caesar went after her, but her short legs went faster than his tired ones. He didn't catch up with her until she'd already reached 41 and his pal, the super-merc.

"Listen to her, Taft," 41 was saying. "She is a good Hawk, well-trained."

"Caesar says you're planning an assault," said Phila. "Exactly what kind? What weapons are you going to deploy from the ground? Do you have air backup? What's the number of your force? Do you have scanners that can be adjusted to register our people's transponder signals? It's no good performing a rescue operation that wipes out the objective."

Taft's red eyes narrowed. He barked an order at the men to reform the column and get moving.

"Hey!" she said more loudly. "I want some answers. You can't just come butting into our mission and screw it up—"

Taft swung at her without warning. But 41 blocked the blow, seizing Taft's wrist and holding it. They stood there a moment, glaring into each other's eyes.

Taft snarled something in merc-speak. 41 answered in kind. Caesar glanced from one to the other, certain they were going to fight. Taft looked like a maniac with his broad face streaked with flage paint and his small eyes glinting. He said something else, something that made the watching mercs snicker and 41 flush.

41 turned and shoved Phila back out of the way. She stumbled into Caesar, who put an arm around her to hold her where she was.

"Let me go!" she said furiously. "That big—"

"Hush," said Caesar, sensing something was wrong.

Taft yelled at the column, and 41 tagged after him with his head down and his fists plainly clenched.

Phila was still struggling in his grip. "No. Dammit, Caesar!"

"Shut up!" he yelled back. He gave her a shake to force some sense into her. In a lower voice, he added, "If you cause much more trouble, they're going to shoot us and Thessic Sazt and leave us for the coscacuns to eat. Put that temper of yours in displacement, Ironpants, and let's stay alive long enough to help Kelly. Agreed?"

Some of the fury went out of her face. She nodded. "Yeah. All right. Just what is going on? Why is 41 doing this to us?"

"I don't know yet," said Caesar as they were shoved into line with Thessic and headed forward across the squelching mud out of the clearing. "I thought he was out for revenge on Kelly. But I'm beginning to think he's not in charge at all. I think Taft is running this show, and he's got snakes for brains."

"That doesn't explain anything," said Phila.

"Well, it's all I know," said Caesar in exasperation. "Yusus, what am I supposed to do? 41 isn't talking. The whole thing is as queer as *postain*. At least we're alive. And as long as we are, we've got a chance."

Phila snorted. "You sound like Kelly. Only he would know what to do."

"Oh, yeah?" said Caesar, stung. "It just so happens Kelly ain't in any shape to know one end of himself from the other. Right now he's probably tweaking, if he's still alive at all."

"What do you mean? He's not—"

"Yes, he is," hissed Caesar. "Tapo."

Her eyes flew wide open. She opened her mouth, closed it, then opened it again. "How did that happen?"

"How do you think?" Caesar was getting madder at her every moment, but he knew it was his own guilt fueling that anger. And he wasn't ready to confess everything to her, not here and now. "The slavers got him on it. Never mind how. So we can't depend on him, do you see?"

Her face puckered with worry. "That means . . . Caesar, he called us on the comm and asked Beaulieu to go into the compound. He claimed the ambassador was injured, but if he's on junk he could be forced to say anything."

"Yeah, well, we got to get him and the doc out, that's all," said Caesar grimly. He stepped into a tangle of vines and nearly tripped. One of the mercs grabbed him by the shoulder and yanked him along. "*Yusus!*" he said, shaking free. "I don't need your help, can-face."

The merc walked on, oblivious to the insult. Caesar glared at him. These giants must have two circuits in their head: one on and one off. And maybe one big brain cell near the base of their spines to regulate bodily functions. Yeah, and their boss Taft was way out on the pole to nowhere. Snakes for brains. Caesar shivered, wondering what it would take to snap Taft's scant control.

"If 41's not running this operation," whispered Phila after several bleak moments of silence, "how are we going to shake loose to carry out our job?"

"I don't know," said Caesar shortly.

"You've got to think of something!"

"Turn over your own brain and see what's under there," he retorted. "It's going to take both of us and all we've got to pull this one off."

"We need 41. Do you think we can turn him back to our side?"

"I don't think 41 knows what being on someone's side means," said Caesar scornfully. "I never have understood what Kelly saw in him anyway."

"We can try."

"I already did."

She sighed and gripped his wrist in the darkness. "I think we're in a hell of a mess, Caesar."

"You got that right," he said.

And fear left a bad taste in his mouth.

12

The ambassador was not going to die. Beaulieu ran her small medi-scanner over Cassandra Caliban's skull for a third time, and studied the readouts with grim satisfaction. The woman had been struck a serious blow that cracked her skull above the left superciliary arch between the frontal eminence and the temporal line. She had bled the usual amount associated with head wounds. There was swelling and some membraneous bruising that concerned Beaulieu initially, but she had dealt with that and there was no longer any danger that a subdural hematoma would form. The ambassador was sedated and settled. She needed absolute quiet and she needed to be transported to a real sickbay facility for additional tests, but otherwise she was in good condition.

"Now for you, Kelly. You look awful."

That was the understatement of the year, she thought. Beneath scabs of dried mud and cinder streaks, his skin was pasty-white. His normally clear blue eyes were bloodshot and filmed over with a haze that could only mean one thing. He was running a low temperature, and wounds in both shoulders were infected. Beaulieu was appalled at his physical condition, but there was no point in saying so.

She began to clean him up, starting first with the infection. The tops of each shoulder were puffy and obviously sore. Angry red streaks across his chest made her frown. She ran her scanner over him.

"You're lucky," she said after a moment, relief making her voice sharp. "The infection hasn't quite reached your heart. And now it won't." She applied antibiotic injections liberally and checked his heartrate again. It remained erratic and too fast. Not good.

Kelly sat there passively, his gaze upon the ambassador, and did not answer. Since Beaulieu had walked into the compound, he had not spoken a single word. He had his hands tucked under his thighs, but she knew that was to hide how badly they were shaking.

It was time to be blunt. "What are you on?" she asked.

No answer. No evidence that he heard her.

She knew he had. "Look, Kelly. This is no time for macho suffering in silence. You're tweaking badly. Fairly soon now you're going to go into some kind of violent withdrawal which will lock you up so that you can't function at all. I can counteract the effects of the addiction, providing I know what I'm up against."

He looked at her. For a moment she thought he was going to speak. Then his jaw clamped tighter than ever. His eyes were wild.

"I interned in a detox ward. It was thirty years ago, but while the names of the junk keeps changing, the effects are pretty much the same. I know what to do. Dammit, Kelly, let me help you!"

He looked away from her, staring at the ambassador who lay there still and silent with a bandage film on her forehead and bloodstains on her cheek. "Help her."

"I have done so. She'll recover."

Relief lit his face. He almost looked like the old Kelly, the one Beaulieu had sworn to follow anywhere. "T-that's great, d-doctor."

Beaulieu frowned in fresh concern. He was disoriented, and that wasn't a good sign. "Kelly, I gave you a full report on her condition less than ten minutes ago. Don't you remember?"

" 'member what?"

"My report."

He blinked a moment, his face blank. Then a wan smile crept to the corners of his eyes. "She'll recover."

"That's right," said Beaulieu in her professional voice. Inside, however, she was swearing. He could start hallucinating, become violent, slip into a coma. What the devil was he on? Dexadrine? Slope? Rostma?

She felt cold and inadequate inside. Any of a dozen drugs could cause this kind of reaction. If it was rostma, and she had to acknowledge that it could well be since they were sitting in the middle of a production plant, she would never get him off it. Rostma was the worst of the lot, the quick killer. It could eat holes in a user's brain in days.

He gripped her hand, startling her. She looked down to see him staring at her with naked want written plainly on his face.

"Doctor," he whispered. "We've got to escape. Get away from Frant. Need a patch. Just one quick hit. Can do the job then. *Please.*"

It was horrible to see Kelly, a man she had always respected, begging like a derelict. The back of her throat constricted, but she pushed her emotions out of the way. This was her chance. "Sure," she said, her voice not quite steady. "We have to escape. We need you to be at your best. What kind of patch?"

He shook his head, a terrible grin spreading across his face. "Clever, clever," he said slyly. "You know. Just one. That's all I need."

"Kelly—" she began.

His gaze shifted past her to her opened medikit. She anticipated his jump for it, but she wasn't strong enough to deflect him. He shoved her to the floor and grabbed the kit. He dumped everything out, his hands scrabbling desperately.

She picked herself up, her hip aching where she'd landed on it. She kicked the kit across the room, momentarily out of his reach. With a hoarse cry he went after it, and she threw herself on his back, getting her arm around his throat in an attempt to stop him.

The door flew open and a guard came in. He brushed Beaulieu aside and scooped Kelly away from the medikit. Slamming Kelly against the wall several times quieted him. Kelly slumped to the floor, not unconscious but dazed. Beaulieu picked up the scattered contents of her kit.

When she straightened, she saw Frant in the doorway. At

once she grew wary. She had seen too many cyborgs become irrational and sometimes psychotic as a result of metal poisoning or the anti-rejection drugs they were forced to take. Bio-engineering accomplished all kinds of wonders, but it could go too far, alter the body too much. She was hardly against the discipline; after all, Commodore West had benefitted from bionic prosthesis. But replacing severely damaged limbs was one thing; substituting good functioning limbs and eyes for augmented replacements was wrong, a moral abuse of science.

"Get Kelly out of here," Frant said to the guard. "Put him with the other workers."

"No!" said Beaulieu. Realizing she was too vehement, she took a swift breath to calm herself and said more reasonably, "If the ambassador awakens, she may be confused and disoriented. Since Kelly was the last one with her before—"

"You want Kelly here so that you may plot an escape with him," said Frant coldly. "You intend to get him off his dependency and functioning again. That will not happen."

"He needs treatment!" snapped Beaulieu.

"He is unimportant." Frant gestured and the guard hauled Kelly to his feet, gave him a good shake and escorted him from the room. "Now," said Frant. "Concentrate on your patient, Doctor. And remember, your life lasts only as long as she stays alive. If she should die, so will you."

Beaulieu had heard threats like that before. She knew the ambassador was out of danger, but she wasn't ready to tell Frant so. If he had this room bugged, he already knew it. If not, he could just worry.

"What about Kelly?" she said. "I demand that you let me treat him. And anyone else who has been injured."

"A noble offer. Some of my guards need care. Elga, my personal assistant, lost a leg and is near death. Would you see to her needs?"

Appalled at Frant's coldness, Beaulieu agreed. Folding her medikit, she stepped forward. "Show me—"

"No, Doctor."

Beaulieu halted. She didn't understand.

"They are all unimportant. We shall have reinforcements soon. Cassandra is the only one you will care for."

"You bastard," said Beaulieu angrily. "What kind of games

are you playing? Are you going to let your assistant die and others suffer when there's no need for it?"

"And what will you do while you tend them?" retorted Frant. "Slip them poison? You came here to destroy us—"

"I'm a physician! I took an oath."

"You are also a StarHawk. You cannot be trusted. Except with this woman's life. She must live."

"She's going to," snapped Beaulieu, past caution. "She's no longer in danger."

Frant lifted his brows, looking surprised. He had the lavender-hued eyes of someone long used to taking tapo as an anti-rejectionant. Eventually, if usage continued long enough, the eyes turned red. Usually the brain went with it, but Frant was a long way from that point. Teletrine was the usual agent prescribed, but it often produced an allergic reaction of its own. She wondered if he knew about phehedrin, a new nonaddictive agent now being tested.

"You are very good at your job," Frant said at last.

"Yes, I am. Now, may I see to—"

"No. You will remain here."

Frant turned and left before Beaulieu could argue further. Frustrated, she went to the locked door and kicked it. So much for her training as an operative. She was supposed to be able to get out of locked rooms, outtalk and outthink her captors, shoot dead straight, and never be at a loss no matter how critical the situation.

A stifled moan came from behind her. Startled, Beaulieu turned and saw that Cassandra was stirring.

She hurried to the young woman's side. "No, don't try to sit up. Lie where you are, Ambassador."

Cassandra opened lovely, gray-flecked eyes and stared at her in bewilderment. "Did I get away?"

"No, I'm afraid not."

Cassandra closed her eyes as though the light hurt them. She frowned. "I don't remember. I was—they were—"

"Easy, easy," said Beaulieu, pressing her down again. "You've had a nasty blow to the head. You need to lie very still and rest."

"Who are you?"

"I'm Antoinette Beaulieu, your doctor." Beaulieu sighed. "And part of the team that is supposed to rescue you."

Cassandra's eyes flew open again. "When—"

"Hold it. Not so fast. We're stuck for the moment. I'm sorry, but I'm as much Frant's prisoner as you are."

"Oh. There was a man with blue eyes. He said he was here to help me—us, I mean. I don't remember—"

"Kelly? Yes. He's my commander."

"Kelly." As she said the name, Cassandra smiled. For a moment Beaulieu caught a glimmer of the charisma that made this woman so beloved by the Zoans. "At first I didn't trust him. But then I found I had to. We were arguing. He wanted me to go through the force wall where I'd be safe. I wanted to help him look for Janitte. Frant caught us. He was going to kill Kelly. I—"

"You're getting far too worked up," said Beaulieu soothingly. She reached for another sedative, although she wasn't ready to put Cassandra out yet. At least now she knew there was no brain damage. Cassandra had straightened out her initial confusion. Her pupils looked good, and she was making perfect sense. No concussion. No blindness. No serious signs of trauma. Beaulieu forced herself to smile. "Don't worry. Kelly is alive. We'll still get out of this."

"You needn't make up lies in an effort to cheer up the patient," said Cassandra. "May I have a drink of water?"

Beaulieu got it for her. "Now I want you to take this and get some sleep. I'll bet your head is really hurting."

"Yes." But Cassandra didn't take the sedative. "Doctor, what about my staff? Have you seen any of them? Do you know about any of them? Their names are—"

"Excuse me, but I know their names and what they look like. We've all been fully briefed." Beaulieu fetched the scanner that was tuned to the transponder signals. "Here, look at this. It's set for the compound. This one is Kelly. This one that's feeding back too sharply is you. And this one belongs to one of your staff. I don't know who. There's one other out in the swamp."

Cassandra frowned in distress. "One is missing. There should be three of mine."

"Yes, I know," said Beaulieu gently. "I'm sorry."

Cassandra handed the scanner back to her. She looked tired. Dark smudges under her eyes and the wan cast to her skin told Beaulieu they had talked long enough. Cassandra said nothing further. She drew away into herself, rather like Kelly did when he lost someone from the squad.

The responsibilities of command, Beaulieu thought grimly. Only Kelly was unable to command in his present state. 41 had deserted them. Siggerson couldn't think beyond the safety of their ship. Caesar was dead. She had checked his signal when she showed the scanner to Cassandra and it still wasn't working. Phila was prowling the perimeters on her own. By now she had little ammunition left and no one to help her. And here Beaulieu sat, like an insect caught in a web, useless to everyone.

Well, she could go on sitting here feeling sorry for herself, or she could start working on a plan of escape. There certainly wasn't going to be any kind of rescue coming her way.

She needed to locate her wristband. If she put that on Cassandra, Siggerson could teleport the ambassador to safety. That was priority one. The trouble was, she hadn't a clue as to where to find it. She did not know the layout of the compound, or what was left of it. She figured Frant had the wristband well secured. Furthermore, Siggerson wasn't due to return to this side of the planet for another hour.

It would be easier to look for Kelly and get him back in working order. If Frant was on tapo, there was a possibility that Kelly was also. She could deal with that.

She checked Cassandra one last time, determined that she was sleeping soundly, then turned her attention to the lock on the door. It was electronic, which meant that if she made a couple of adjustments on her medi-scanner, modified by the technicians at Allied Intelligence, she could quickly break the code.

Before she did so, however, she prepared a quick-hit hypo for the guard, praying there was only one on the other side of the door. Then she broke the code lock, pocketed her scanner, and eased open the door.

There was only one guard as she'd hoped, but he was alert. He was already turning with his hand reaching for his weapon. She jabbed him with the hypo. He howled and shot at her, catching her in the shoulder with a stun that sent her sprawling back into the room.

The guard wrenched open the door and aimed his weapon at her a second time as she lay there helpless and gasping. Then a strange look crossed his face. He swayed, dropping his weapon, and crumpled.

Beaulieu writhed on the floor, battling her acute nausea, and tried to sit up. She knew she had barely been clipped by the stun, but just the same, the misery involved was almost incapacitating. She levered herself to her knees, trying to hold back her gasps of wretchedness. A clammy sweat broke out over her.

She picked up the guard's weapon with her good hand and searched him for his communicator, force wall key, and other weapons. She considered dragging him out of the doorway, but his absence as a guard would be noted whether he was left sprawled where he was or hidden. She didn't think she had it in her to move him.

"Damn!" she said through her teeth and made it onto her feet.

Staggering like a drunk, she stepped over him and went down a short corridor past another closed door to a sort of airlock that was obviously used to conserve the air conditioning.

Outside, the dank, warm air smothered her. She paused in the shadows to rest.

The compound was not as well-lit as she had expected it to be. They were conserving energy perhaps. It left plenty of thick dark shadows to hide in, which was good, but it also left her dubious about finding Kelly, which was not.

She listened, hearing muffled voices in the distance, the irregular throb of generators, the almost inaudible whine of the force wall, and the raucous cries and screams of the jungle life beyond. She headed toward the voices.

Her boots crunched on charred pieces of debris. Smoke still thickened the air. Now and then she danced over a patch of ground that glowed orange with live embers, feeling the intense heat through her soles.

A repair crew was working on the far side of the compound. Lights shone there. She gave that area a wide berth. Altogether, there wasn't much left standing: the modular unit she'd left, one quick-set too small to hold the labor force, and a cluster of makeshift tents.

It began to rain, turning the ashes on the ground to lye. Drenched in seconds, Beaulieu welcomed the downpour. Its noise would help mask her movements better. She headed for the tents.

They were long and narrow, not tall enough for a person to walk upright inside, and lined up end to end. Two guards stood at each entrance. There were no exits. She went to the first one and crept around to the side. With the rain thrumming on her back, she crouched there and cut a slit with her laser scapel. Then she eased inside into a sticky, foul-smelling fog of unwashed bodies, swamp mud, and sickness.

She paused, overwhelmed by so much misery and suffering packed together. There was no floor. They lay directly on the muddy ground. Pulling herself together, she began her search, going from one to the next, shining her micro-torch briefly on faces. No one protested or even stirred. They were in an uncaring stupor. Some of them were drugged. Others were simply exhausted past endurance. She saw malnutrition, raw sores, leech bites, cuts, bruises, skin fungus, mange, untreated burns, tremors, and other maladies too numerous to mention. She wanted to sweep every single one of these creatures into a disinfectant bath and proceed with treatment, but she forced down her anger and outrage and kept herself focused on the objective at hand.

Kelly was not in the first tent, or the second. She found him in the third, semi-conscious and convulsing. Frightened, cursing the darkness, the need for stealth, and her own awkward one-handedness, she fumbled and gave him an injection. This was hardly standard detox procedure, but in this kind of emergency she was ready to throw her professional scruples aside.

His convulsions stopped. But there he lay. How was she going to get him out? She dared risk another shine of her torch. The light reflected off his open eyes. Not even a shift of response. If he went into coma, she might as well give up. She couldn't get him out of here unless he walked or crawled on his own power.

She gave him a shake. "Kelly," she whispered in his ear. "Kelly! Come on, try. We've got to get out of here. Kelly!"

Nothing.

She pressed her hand to his chest, feeling it rise and fall. Exhaustion weighed her down. She had come this far, but it just wasn't good enough. The stun was wearing off and a slight amount of feeling was returning to her left arm, but she barely noticed. Tears stung her eyes, and their uselessness made her angry.

"Kelly!" she whispered. "Damn you, don't quit on me now! We need you."

But Kelly didn't stir.

13

The mercenary force now ringed the compound. Armed with heavy-duty ack rifles, flame throwers, launchers, and the element of surprise, they had only to begin. In less than thirty minutes, Caesar was sure, they could level what remained of the compound. And destroy every living being inside the force walls as well.

Caesar lay belly flat in the mud, his head stuck through a bush. Phila crouched beside him. Thessic muttered soft, incomprehensible things to himself. Maybe they were prayers. Caesar figured with the massacre about to commence, somebody needed to say prayers.

"This stinks," he whispered to Phila. "Stinks like last year's laundry. We can't get to Kelly and the others. We aren't even armed except for my little bombs, and they aren't exactly good for hand-to-hand fighting."

"Once they cut down the force wall," said Phila, "we must still go inside. We must try."

"Yo, but which do you want to be?" retorted Caesar. "Crisped or minced? I ain't fond of suicide jumps, toots."

"I guess you're saying that we should just sit here and do nothing. You—"

Hearing a rustle nearby, Caesar gripped her wrist very hard to silence her. The quiet footsteps came toward them, and within moments a dim shape squatted in front of the bush where Caesar and Phila were taking cover. Caesar wondered if the merc knew they were here or not. If not, he could jump the brawnoid and get his weapons. Then they would . . .

"Caesar," said 41 quietly. "You and Phila heed me. We have only—"

Caesar sat up, disentangling his head from the branches. "Why should we listen to a damned traitor like you? If it weren't for you, we wouldn't—"

41 could still move faster than thought. Before Caesar knew what was happening, or could defend himself, 41 had him by the throat. He applied just enough pressure to make Caesar dizzy.

"Shut up," he said almost inaudibly, yet the menace in his voice warned Caesar to obey. "I have gained for us fifteen minutes. We cannot waste that time arguing among ourselves."

He released Caesar, and Caesar angrily rubbed his throat. "Fifteen minutes for what? Holding a memorial service for Kelly before your pals blow the place sky high?"

Instead of answering, 41 shoved an object into his hands. Caesar fumbled and nearly dropped the pistol in his shock.

"Yusus!" he said in surprise. "How did you—"

He shut himself up while 41 supplied Phila with his laser wings and a small device that she held up.

"What's this?" she asked.

"Force wall key," said 41. "We'll use it to get in. It's blackmarket, very expensive. Don't lose it. Also, this." He handed her something else.

"The scanner," she said in excitement. She thrust the key at Caesar and switched on the scanner. "Got 'em!"

41's head bent over hers. "Show me."

Caesar and Thessic also crowded up as she began to explain.

"Hokay, this blip and this blip are Zoans. Slight difference in frequency from our transponders."

"Thanks be that the ambassador is safe," said Thessic.

"Unimportant," said 41. "Where is Kelly?"

"Unimportant?" said Thessic in a furious squeak. "How dare you—"

Caesar squeezed his shoulder to make him be quiet. "We'll get all of them. Stop squawking."

"This is Kelly," said Phila. "He's maybe twenty meters distant from one of the Zoans. The other blip, as you can see, is almost half the compound away. That will make it harder."

"What about Beaulieu?" asked Caesar.

"She isn't wearing a transponder. Neither am I," replied Phila. "But it's a sure bet that she's in one of these three locations."

"She will be with Kelly," said 41.

"Not necessarily," said Phila. "Remember that she went in there to tend the ambassador's injuries."

"Can the scanner be set to isolate one signal?"

Phila hesitated. "Yes," she said at last. "But I think it's better to keep it on this setting where we can get a general bearing on everyone's placement."

"Set it for Kelly," said 41. "Caesar, use the key. We now have thirteen minutes."

Caesar rose to his feet. "Not just yet. What exactly are you up to, 41?"

"Caesar, what difference does it make?" demanded Phila urgently. "We are running out of time."

"It makes a lot of difference," said Caesar. "We have orders to get the Zoans out. That's why we came here and risked our necks in the first place. We aren't here just to save our own butts."

"You can get the Zoans," said 41. "I am going after Kelly."

He turned away, but Caesar blocked his path. "Why? To kill him?"

41 drew in his breath audibly. In that instant Caesar could feel his rage. Caesar braced himself, ready for a fight. In fact he *wanted* a fight, wanted the satisfaction of planting his fist in 41's teeth and showing the big, half-breed bastard what loyalty was all about.

"Eleven minutes," said Phila in a moan. "Come on, you two! We can settle this later."

She snatched the key from Caesar's hand and scuttled toward the force wall in a half crouch. 41 followed, and with a muttered oath Caesar went along, dissatisfied and as suspicious as hell.

The key wasn't quite on the correct setting, but Phila knew

how to make a circuit go her way. In seconds, she had a
blue-tinged waver in the field. She stuck her hand through to
test it, then gestured impatiently.

41 was the first one through. He did a shoulder roll, came
onto his feet, and hit a run. Caesar blundered after him,
tripping on the edge of the waver and getting a shock up his leg
that numbed him. Hobbling and cursing under his breath, he
pulled himself upright.

"Phila, head for the Zoans."

She pulled off the key and ducked through the split-second
lag time before the force wall closed again. "What about you?"

"I'm keeping an eye on 41," said Caesar grimly. "I don't
trust him as far as I can throw him."

She said something he didn't hear. He was already running,
his feet squelching so loudly he feared guards would come
looking for him any moment. A downpour started falling,
obliterating the world. He could barely see in the minimum
lighting anyway. 41 was too far ahead of him, flitting like a
shadow, silent and deadly. Grimly Caesar did his best to
follow.

41 began by heading for one of the huts, but he abruptly
veered. Caesar didn't understand why until 41 disappeared
from sight. Panicked, Caesar quickened his speed although he
was already going too fast for caution.

At the last second he spotted the tents and slewed to a stop
behind a melted lump of something indefinable. He crouched
there, his breath choking in his throat, and prayed that the
guards outside the tents hadn't seen him. There was no outcry,
and after a few moments Caesar let out his breath with a little
sob of relief.

41 had gone that way, but he wasn't in sight now. Which
tent? Caesar peered around the edge of his hiding place.
Through the blur of rain and darkness, he counted four. With
his headstart, 41 could have a knife through Kelly's throat
before Caesar ever got there.

He got to his feet, knowing that if he had to search every
damned tent, he would. But just as he eased out, a squad of
guards emerged from the nearby modular unit.

The light spilling from the opened doorway illuminated one
man. Seeing the flash of pale hair, Caesar recognized Frant and
stiffened in hatred. He brought up his pistol, aiming it right at

him. One shot, and Frant would never run another slave camp.

Just before he could fire, however, reason returned to him. Caesar knew that if he killed Frant, the whole compound would erupt. For a moment he didn't care, then he forced himself to lower the pistol.

Kelly's voice, from a long-ago training lecture, returned to his memory: "If you can't keep yourself a cut above the enemy, then you have no place in the Hawks. They will use every vicious, cutthroat trick in the book, but if you take expediency over principle, you're as bad as they are and you have no right to hunt them down."

Caesar blew out a deep breath. He wanted to kill Frant so bad it hurt. No, not just Frant, but all of them and what they stood for. His only sister, five years older, had died of an overdose on the recreational drug called Slope. It wasn't even supposed to be dangerous. She used to say she liked the kick it gave her. But it was a long way down, and finally Lisal took it. Somewhere along the way, he'd forgotten Lisal, shoved her to the back of his mind. He wasn't like Phila, who based her life on vendetta. But he guessed that somehow Lisal was the reason he had joined the StarHawks. Right now he wanted Frant to pay for Lisal, and for Kelly, and for all the victims.

One clear shot. But he couldn't fire.

In the rain, it was several moments before he realized tears were streaming down his cheeks. He wiped his face although the rain was washing them away.

"Ah, hell," he whispered.

And by then someone stood between him and Frant.

"How the doctor got out of the ambassador's room doesn't matter. She's bound to have gone to the workers. Search the tents," said Frant.

Wildly Caesar looked that way. The guards were already going in that direction. He couldn't warn 41. He couldn't get to Kelly.

But he could carry out his job. He waited until Frant turned away from the unit. Then he raced across the open space and flung himself up the steps and into the unit.

The light inside blinded him. He gasped, water streaming off him, and quickly checked the charge on his pistol to be sure 41 had given him a weapon that worked. It did work, and the charge was full. Caesar bared his teeth, leaving his mouth open to get air faster.

He went down the short corridor. Two doors, neither guarded. He tried one and found it unlocked. Sliding it open a fraction, he heard the hum of equipment. He went on hastily to the other one. It was locked.

Caesar shot out the lock, sending torn circuits spitting and frying. He kicked in the door and burst inside only to come up short at the sight of a beautiful young woman lying on a bunk. Her auburn hair spilled over the pillow nearly to the floor. Caesar went weak in the knees. His heart thudded hard against his ribs. Her holos hadn't done her justice. This lady was one knockout.

His entry awakened her. She put a hand to her forehead where a flesh-colored bandage film looked too shiny to be real skin.

"Who—" she began groggily.

He stepped forward and helped her sit up. "I'm your rescue, babe. Uh, I mean, ma'am. Come on now. We don't have much time. Think you can walk?"

She rubbed her forehead again. "I have an awful headache," she said. "But I'll try."

"Yo," he said steadying her. "Lean on me. We'll take it easy, but if we don't get out of here now, there ain't going to be no tomorrow."

"I understand."

She took a couple of tottery steps, swayed, and Caesar had to slip his arm around her to keep her on her feet.

It didn't matter that she was taller than he. She was built with everything a woman should have.

"That's it. You're doing fine," he said.

"I'm sorry. I'm so dizzy."

But she kept trying, much to his relief, and they finally made it to the door. He knew that if she ever collapsed on him, he wouldn't be able to carry her and fight his way out too.

"Down the hall and outside we go," he said, keeping up a steady patter of encouragement. She kept melting on him, and he kept standing her up again. He dreaded taking her outside into the rain, but it seemed to help wake her up.

He pulled her into the shadows as quickly as possible, but a shout told him they'd been seen.

Caesar pressed his back against the building with a groan of despair. He couldn't run with her. He couldn't bounce her around with a head injury. And any second now the mercs were going to open fire. This would be a battle zone, and Cassandra wouldn't have a chance of getting out of it alive.

"Ma'am? Uh, ma'am?" he said. He hadn't called anyone that since his mother died. He felt like a fool, but it couldn't be helped. "Can you get yourself down to the corner and around to the back of this unit?"

She looked at the pistol in his hand. "Yes," she said and slowly, using the building for support, inched away from him into the darkness.

The guard came blundering into Caesar's line of fire. Caesar shot him between the eyes, and then killed the man following him. He dragged them both into the shadows, then started after Cassandra.

Maybe, he thought with renewed optimism, they could make it after all.

But just as he caught up with her, a blinding flash of flamethrower reflecting off the force wall warned him that their grace period was over.

He stared with horror, then threw himself at her. "Get down!" he yelled.

She went sprawling, and Caesar barely had time to crawl on top of her for protection before the whole world blew up.

Phila figured out pretty quickly that she was heading for the refinery. Or rather, what was left of it. The remaining buildings and quick-sets had been pulled to the north side of the compound as far away from the ruined refinery as possible. That was probably to avoid rostma contamination. Phila quickened her pace, but she worried. She didn't want to breathe the stuff or get it on her skin if she could help it. She hoped rain nullified it, but she'd better not count on that.

Although she made sure she kept well under cover, she saw no guards on this side. Yet her scanner continued to show her one of the Zoan blips. Where?

When she got close enough to the charred ruins of the refinery, she squinted through the driving rain and saw a huddle of individuals crouched on the ground. They didn't move, but her scanner told her that they were alive.

She approached warily, tucking away her scanner and drawing out her laser wing instead. She wished she had a pistol. In her left hand, she snapped out all three blades of her prong, which the mercenaries hadn't taken from her. Thus armed, she crept up to the workers and found that they were held in place by activated fusion shackles which had frozen their limbs into a crouch.

"*Vita mandale*," she said in disgust. She didn't have a torch, and she couldn't tell one face from another in the gloom. There wasn't even lightning to give her intermittent illumination.

"Janitte? Ambassador?" she called softly, moving from one to another.

Some of them mumbled, but not in response. She leaned closer and got fetid breath blown in her face. One had toppled over in the mud, arms and legs still frozen, and had apparently drowned in a shallow puddle. Most were women or youths. Obviously they were what remained of the refinery workers. All were obviously suffering from rostma addiction. None seemed able to respond to her.

"Janitte Krensky? Ambassador Caliban?"

Her scanner was useless at this range. The feedback was too strong, and she could not adjust it without losing the signal entirely.

She went on searching, trying not to count the fleeing minutes.

In desperation, she paused and fumbled in her mind for the scant amount of Zoan she knew. She drew a deep breath, certain her pronunciation was wrong.

"*Ardoi d'ounie sin creiti*?"

One figure lifted her head. "*Chu.*"

Phila ran to her in relief. The woman was middle-aged, with the flabby look of having recently lost considerable weight. Phila gripped her shoulder.

"Janitte Krensky?" she said.

No answer. The whites of the woman's eyes glimmered in the shadows. Phila crouched beside her and went to work shorting out her shackles.

"Hang on. We'll have you free in just a moment."

A boy sitting nearby turned his head. "You're going to leave us," he said in a peculiar, extremely clear voice. "You're going to leave us to die. We'll die in a great rush of fire, as some of us did this afternoon. It is a judging upon this place."

A chill went through Phila. Rostma was supposed to make its victims telepathic. Was this boy reading her mind? It didn't matter, because he was right.

She finished freeing Janitte and stood up. She felt sorry for the rest of them who were trapped here, soon to die. Maybe she could free some of them, give them a chance, but no, there wasn't time.

"Come on, Janitte," she said, tugging at the woman, who was still crouched in the mud. "We have to go now. The ambassador wants you."

Janitte slowly tilted her head to look up at Phila.

Encouraged that she had reached through the fog, Phila extended her hand. "Come," she said.

Janitte clasped her hand with fingers surprisingly strong. She rose to her feet, but when Phila walked away she did not follow.

Phila hurried back. "Come *on*. We haven't much time. The ambassador needs you right away."

Janitte began to laugh deep in her throat. She raised her hands to the rain, letting it sluice over her. "I'm dead. I'm dead," she sang. "Look at my hands. I can see through my hands."

Consternation ran through Phila. She grabbed Janitte's wrists and pulled them down. "No," she said gently, tugging. "We're going to get you help. Come. Please come."

Janitte started walking, and in relief Phila clung to her hand in an effort to keep her going. They were only fifty or so meters from the force wall at this point. Not far. They could make it.

Janitte stumbled. Quickly Phila put an arm around her to keep her from falling. Their bodies bumped, and suddenly Janitte's hands were grabbing and pounding. Taken by surprise, Phila dropped her laser wing and had to kick it into the darkness to keep Janitte from getting it.

Janitte grabbed her by the throat and began to shake her from side to side. Phila's feet skidded in the mud. She couldn't plant to give herself leverage. Instead, she kicked high and hard, catching Janitte in the midsection.

With a whompf, Janitte went sprawling, but her hands clung like claws to Phila and pulled her down with her. Phila squirmed desperately and managed at last to break free of that stranglehold.

She rolled out of reach, her breath wheezing in her throat. *Don't pass out*, she told herself fiercely, struggling to recover. Somehow she managed to get to her knees. She felt dangerously light-headed, but her wind was coming back.

Janitte faced her, crouching as though to spring.

"Enough of this," Phila said sternly. "You're coming with me quietly, Janitte. No more nonsense."

Janitte laughed again with the heedless, wild mirth of insanity. And beneath the sound, Phila heard the soft, unmistakable snick of a prong blade sliding into position. Her breath seemed to lodge in her throat. She didn't remember dropping it.

But Janitte had it.

To the east, an explosion rocked the compound, lighting up the place with a fierce orange glow. In that split second, Phila realized her time was up. If she didn't get out of the compound now, she was finished.

She also saw Janitte clearly, saw the slack, out-of-shape body that had the strength of madness. She saw Janitte's staring eyes, saw the dark slash of her mouth. Janitte was laughing, singing to herself, and calling out in a mixture of Zoan and Glish.

"Janitte! Come with me to help Cassandra."

Janitte met Phila's gaze. For an instant there was anguish—mute and intelligent—to be seen in her face. Then the madness seized her again. She swung the knife high and came at Phila.

Kelly awakened to a touch on his face. He had been deeply unconscious, yet in an instant his mind was clear and cognizant. He drew a deep breath and opened his eyes. In the dim light of a micro-torch, he saw 41's face hanging over him.

41 let out his breath audibly, as though he had been holding it. His fingers slid away from Kelly's temple.

Kelly thought, *It's a dream. I've gone over the edge. I'm hallucinating.*

"There is not much time," said 41. "The guards know the doctor is missing. They are searching the first tent now."

In the distance, Kelly could hear a faint commotion: shouted orders, thin cries of denial, screams of pain. Kelly did not have a clear idea of where he was. But something in his subconscious obviously understood 41, for Kelly found himself nodding. He tried to sit up, but everything spun around him.

41 gripped his arms and sat him up as one would a child. "I can carry you if necessary," he whispered. "But to walk is better."

Kelly nodded again, but he did not move. He stared at 41's face. It looked tired and harassed. "How did you get here?" he asked in wonderment.

"Later," said Beaulieu in a loud whisper. "They're going through the second tent. We have to get out *now*."

"We can't talk," said 41. His amber eyes bored into Kelly's. He gripped Kelly's hand. "Come."

In sudden anger Kelly slapped his hand away. "No. You betrayed us. Sold us out to Frant—"

"No," said Beaulieu hastily as 41 stiffened. "No, Kelly. That was Nash. He gave us away to Frant, and he tried to steal the *Sabre* to trade it for the ambassador. 41 is here to help you."

Relief flooded Kelly. He slumped back. "Didn't want it to be 41," he mumbled.

"Come," said 41. "You cannot sleep now. You must come."

With 41's help, Kelly got to his feet, only to find he had to bend nearly double in the low tent. He staggered along after Beaulieu, who kept hurrying ahead, picking a path through the sleeping workers, then turning back and reaching out to him to hurry him along. Kelly understood that they were in danger, that it was urgent that they get away, yet the rest of him remained detached and unconcerned. He did not particularly want to hurry, but he tried because they wanted it so much.

Ducking out through the slit in the tent was almost too much for him. He sank to his knees and 41 hauled him up again. With Beaulieu on his other side, they hustled him along into the shadows just seconds before the guards entered the third tent. 41 shoved Kelly behind a charred stack of something that smelled unpleasant. The three of them crouched there in a huddle while the guards emerged swearing and ran to the last tent.

"Now," said 41.

They ran, darting from pile to pile of what Kelly finally realized were ruined rostma stacks. Running was more like floating. He couldn't feel his feet, only his head. It was almost pleasant.

Then he tripped and fell flat with a jarring impact. It drove out the clarity which he realized was false. In its place came a rush of aching misery, pain, and need like a fire in his veins. He remembered with shame and self-disgust.

Addict."

"Kelly."

41 and Beaulieu were lifting him out of the mud, standing him up. He shook himself free of their helping hands and glanced around, squinting through a world made askew by rain, until he spied the unit where Cassandra remained a prisoner.

"Got to help her," he said. His tongue was suddenly thick and uncooperative. He raged at it, at his own disgusting helplessness. And the anger brought him enough strength to hold 41 at arm's length. "Go back for Cassandra."

"No," said 41. "I came to help you. No other."

"I am not important. She is."

41 glanced over his shoulder at the unit where lights blazed everywhere. "Caesar is with her. He can do the job."

"Caesar!" cried Beaulieu. "He's alive?"

"Good," said Kelly, paying her no heed. "Go and help him. Beaulieu and I can manage."

"No," said 41. He tried to propel Kelly forward.

Kelly fought him off, flailing until he lost his balance. Only 41's quick grab saved him from falling again. Kelly sagged against 41's chest, his breath sobbing raggedly in his throat.

"Dammit, 41," he said weakly. "Do what I ask. We have our mission to carry out—"

"I will not serve your destruction!" said 41. "I told you this before."

"Then why the hell are you here?" asked Kelly.

They looked at each other a long moment. Kelly broke from the support of 41's arm. He stood unsteadily while Beaulieu made little motions of impatience.

"I am the mission," said Kelly. "It's what I do. It's what I am. If I fail, that is destruction too."

"You are wrong. You are foolish."

"I can't help that," said Kelly. "It's how I'm put together."

"For God's sake, you two!" yelled Beaulieu as though she'd

forgotten about caution. "Will you do something besides stand here?"

Kelly went on looking at 41. He had to make him understand, yet his moment of energy ran out on him and he could not continue the argument. "41," he said quietly with the last of his strength.

41 pushed past him and faced Beaulieu. "There are heavily armed mercenaries surrounding the compound. In less than two minutes from now, they are going to open fire. Take this." He handed Beaulieu a small object. "It is a force wall key. Get Kelly out."

She closed her hand over the key. "My God," she breathed. "What are you—"

41 turned away from her and came back to Kelly.

"I shall do what you ask, but in return you must get out alive. Swear to me, on your blood, on your rank, on your family honor."

Kelly was aghast at what he'd done. If this compound was destroyed by the force 41 had assembled, then he'd just asked his friend to remain and be destroyed in it. His throat choked up.

"41—"

"*Swear*, Kelly!"

"On my honor as—as an officer and a gentleman," said Kelly unsteadily. "41—"

41 spun him around and gave him a push toward Beaulieu. "Go. Go!"

"Thank you," whispered Kelly.

But 41 was already hurrying away. It was doubtful that he heard.

Kelly stood there, anguished and torn. "My God," he said. "What have I done?"

"What you had to do, as a commanding officer in charge of a damnfool mission without adequate forces or backup," said Beaulieu grimly. She took his arm. "Come on, Commander. You've got a promise to keep."

14

The first barrage from the east started while Beaulieu was fumbling with the key. She dropped it, hunted frantically in the darkness for it, picked it up, and slapped it on the wall again.

"Now work, dammit!" she said. "Work!"

A waver began to form.

Kelly glanced back. "I can't do this," he said. "Caesar, 41, and probably Phila as well are all back there—"

"This isn't ancient Sparta," said Beaulieu grimly. "You don't have to come back with your shield or on it. Be reasonable, Kelly! You don't have a weapon. You can barely walk. In a few more minutes what I gave you is going to wear off. The waver is ready. Go through."

"You first," said Kelly without thinking.

She shook her head. "Oh, no. I know you too well. You're planning on getting rid of me and doubling back. It won't work. Come on."

"I'm not just going to sit on my thumbs and do nothing to help them!"

"You've done all you can do. Don't blunder back where you can't help. You'll only be in their way. You could jeopardize everything."

It was blunt, harsh, and true. Kelly knew he had no choice but to acquiesce.

But he still felt rotten about it.

Awkwardly he sank to his knees and crawled through the waver. It made him queasy, but he came out on the other side. Beaulieu started through, but he saw a shape approaching out of the rain.

"Doctor!" he said in alarm. "Hurry!"

"Not so fast," said Frant's voice. "I have a laser-scoped pistol aimed at the fourteenth vertebra of Dr. Beaulieu's spine. Don't try anything foolish."

The barrage intensified, bringing with it the unmistakable chuffs and pops of charges going up. The force wall crackled and rippled around the waver Beaulieu was still holding open. She stood frozen, staring as Frant came into view.

Kelly got somehow to his feet. All he needed was a gun. But he was helpless. Frustration burned inside him. Where were those mercenaries? Why couldn't one come along now and get them out of this?

"Give me the key," said Frant.

Without a word Beaulieu surrendered it to him. He pressed it once again to the wall, recreating the waver. "After you, Doctor," he said.

She glanced at Kelly and ducked quickly through. Frant followed with the ease of long practice. The force wall closed behind him, then long, vicious whips of blue energy lines spread through it with a violence that sent all three of them scrambling into the cover of the jungle. The force wall collapsed, and as though that was a signal, the attack commenced from all sides.

Kelly threw himself flat, covering his ears. They had to be within twenty meters of a short cannon by the sheer volume of noise. But he couldn't see the operator in this jungle.

The darkness was now lit by a steady glow of fire and explosion. Running figures were silhouetted momentarily, only to disappear in the next blast. Mud and debris flew through the air. Smoke boiled everywhere. Evil and thick, it was another kind of weapon that brought down its own victims.

Kelly raised himself to look, then he could not tear his gaze away. The men and women who ran pell mell were completely disorganized. It was wholesale slaughter. No one in the compound had the slightest hope of fighting back, or of surviving.

Enraged, Kelly pushed himself to his knees. "Stop!" he yelled, although in the noise no one could hear him. He looked around. He had to find the operator of that short cannon and put an end to this barbarism.

But Frant was in front of him, the weapon steady in his hand. "You aren't running away, Kelly. There's no need now. You've won."

Sickened, Kelly gestured at what was happening. "Is this a victory?"

"It is my defeat. I've lost my job."

"Your men are dying. Don't you care?"

Beaulieu touched his arm. "Easy, Kelly. Calm down."

Kelly paid her no heed. His anger was a heat that throbbed through him like the artillery blasts. He could feel it roaring through his ears, blazing in his face. He glared at Frant, loathing this creature who could remain icily cool at a time like this, who could even joke about it.

"My men?" said Frant, a glimmer of a smile playing upon his pale lips. "No, they are Mechtaxlan's men. I am merely their highly paid supervisor. And you are now my ticket off Kenszana. As long as I'm alive, I can find other employers. But I don't intend to rot in this miserable swamp until someone from the cartel decides to come looking for me. Where is your ship? What is its call frequency?"

Kelly stared at him and felt a shiver of exhaustion, then another. Beaulieu was right. Whatever she'd given him was wearing off right on schedule. *Not yet*, he told himself fiercely.

"Go to hell, Frant," he said.

"I've been there," said Frant. He held up a wristband. "This was a little bauble we took off Dr. Beaulieu. It contains a teleport signal as well as a communicator, I believe. I have been calling for pickup, but without response. Therefore I must not be on the correct frequency. Tell me which one."

"Why should I?" said Kelly. "Why should I give you my ship?"

"Because your friends blasting this miserable place to bits will take care of you. And if you don't tell me, I am going to kill the doctor."

The muzzle of his gun swung toward Beaulieu.

Her eyes widened. Then she grew very stiff and dignified. "Death is a risk we're prepared to take when we sign on," she said.

"But Kelly is such a compassionate commander," said Frant. His lavender eyes challenged Kelly's. "He would much rather die himself than see one of his operatives die." Frant squeezed the trigger and the gun went off.

Beaulieu was knocked sprawling, her cry of pain shrill even above the thunder of the short cannon.

Blind rage seized Kelly. He forgot the danger, his own weakness, forgot everything except the desire to put an end to Frant once and for all. Without thinking, he launched himself at Frant. The tackle was too short, but it did tip Frant off balance.

They fell together into the undergrowth, kicking and pummeling each other. Frant hit him with an augmented fist in the short ribs, driving all the air from Kelly's lungs.

Wheezing, Kelly felt the strength sag from him. He was furious at being so weak, but fury did him no good. Frant hit him again for good measure, sending a starburst of agony through Kelly's side, then kicked free of him and stood up.

"Now, StarHawk," said Frant, standing over him. He aimed his weapon at Kelly's throat. "You have a choice. You can give me the frequency I want. You can even come with me. Join me. The two of us are very alike, you know. Now that you have a taste of the life, you would make a good man for the cartel."

Kelly managed to drag in enough breath to answer. "You want me to join the cartel? Work for men who live off the sick degradation of others?"

Frant laughed. "Don't sound so offended, Kelly. It's money. Unbelievable amounts of money. And when you begin to see the power and the freedom that money gives you, where it comes from ceases to matter. Come on, Kelly! Don't be a fool."

He held out the wristband. Slowly, wincing and holding his broken ribs, Kelly somehow climbed to his feet. He had to prop himself against a tree to stay upright. Frant doubled, then tripled. Kelly blinked fiercely to clear his vision, and all the Frants became one again. Mutely Kelly reached out, and Frant put the wristband upon his palm.

The way home.

Kelly frowned in startlement at that thought, so forceful, so clear inside his head as though it had been thrown at him. He glanced up and saw Frant staring at him with an odd intensity.

"The way home, Kelly," said Frant.

Kelly went cold inside. If Frant could put thoughts into his head, was he reading them?

"If I joined up with you, Frant, I'd be dead in a week."

"Perhaps. I think you're too smart to let that happen, however. Enough stalling, Kelly. I've offered you a way out. I don't know where these mercenaries came from, but they mean neither of us any good. Your only chance is with me. Now. What's it to be?"

Kelly bowed his head. Slowly, he put the wristband on. He checked the settings. Slowly he brought it up to his mouth.

"No tricks!" said Frant. He held up his own left wrist. "I am wearing a band also. The doctor carried this spare in her pocket. For the ambassador, I'm sure. Now speak carefully, Kelly. We both go up, or you die."

Kelly barely heard the threat. He was thinking of Beaulieu sprawled face down in the mud. Rage at the senseless futility of her death, of 41, Caesar, Cassandra, and Phila all mowed down inside the compound, tore at him. He wanted to tell Frant what to do with his offer, but he held onto his emotions with an iron fist. If he ever let go, there would be no coming back.

Again he lifted his wrist to his mouth. "Kelly to *Sabre*," he said. He waited, holding his wrist there. And in the cover of the shadows, he stuck his thumb into his mouth, running it along his upper molars to the single, tiny bomb Caesar had insisted he bring along. He inserted his thumbnail in the small crack and pried the bomb halfway loose.

"Kelly to *Sabre*."

"This is *Sabre*," said Siggerson's voice, sounding very far away. "We hear you, Kelly. How much longer are you going to be down there? I'm trying to effect repairs to the—"

"Stand by for orders," said Kelly.

Siggerson sighed. "Standing by."

As soon as Siggerson began to reply, Frant leaned forward to listen. Less than two meters separated him from Kelly, too close, yet there was no choice.

Kelly worked the bomb all the way loose with his tongue and spat it into his palm.

"Tell him!" said Frant. "Tell him to bring us up."

"Uh, Siggerson," said Kelly. His head felt very cool, as though the fever had finally burned itself out. Only his pulse went on thumping too fast in his temples. He found himself short of breath. "Are you reading my coordinates?"

"Affirmative."

"As soon as they're locked in, teleport us—"

Without finishing his sentence, Kelly threw the tiny bomb at Frant. It hit him in the chest, and for a split second Kelly thought nothing was going to happen. Maybe too much saliva had defused it or he hadn't set the detonator correctly. All this time he'd been walking around terrified that he would chew wrong and blow his head off, and it wasn't going to do a—

The blast was brief but vicious. Kelly felt a swift suck of air around him, then it came back at him like a punch in the face, throwing him backward. At the same time, he heard a flat clap of a sound that didn't seem loud enough to be deafening, yet was. As he fell, the noise of the short cannon, the launchers, and the rest of the artillery ceased. The silence hurt. Yet he was glad of it. Being deaf was a small price to pay for ending Frant's career.

Then he hit the ground and heard his muffled ooph of pain and the crackle of snapped twigs beneath him. He knew then that he wasn't deaf. The fighting had stopped. It was over.

The impact of hitting the ground hurt, and suddenly everything hurt. He could have passed out from the sheer grinding misery of too many aches and bruises, his broken ribs, his infection, that horrible wretched *need* that scared him as much as it made him feel ashamed.

Besides, if he was the only one who survived and came home—without his shield—as Beaulieu had so quaintly phrased it, then he didn't think it was going to be worth much. And he didn't think he could go on being a Hawk. Someone else would have to take on the tough, impossible jobs. Someone else would have to shoulder the responsibility.

"Kelly?"

The voice was faint. Thinking it was Siggerson, Kelly touched his comm. He waited. No one spoke. With a sigh, Kelly let his arm drop. He closed his eyes.

"Kelly?"

Again he touched his comm. This time, however, he realized the voice was here, nearby, not a transmission. Wearily he sat up, wincing at the stitch in his side. He waited, but the voice did not call his name again.

He got onto his knees and hitched himself along that way. The ground would be too far away if he got to his feet. He wanted the ground to be close, in case he fell again. He was getting tired of falling. Falling hurt.

"Kelly? Wherezit?"

He found Beaulieu, still face down in the mud, making aimless gropings with her hands and mumbling. He touched her with a hand that shook. Her face was cold, except where the blood trickled down. His fingers dug into her shoulder with a relief so intense it hurt him.

He tilted back his head and let his tears blur the constellations now shining through the dissipating cloud cover. "Antoinette," he said. He said her name many times, as though saying it would anchor her more firmly to life.

Footsteps came squelching toward him. He looked and it was an unfamiliar giant of a figure that approached. A figure that came up and shone a torch over him and Beaulieu. She'd been creased in the head. He kept his palm curled around her throat where he could feel her pulse throbbing against his skin.

"I have one," he said. "One left. I have one."

The giant remained in darkness behind the glare of the torch. "You are crazy. I do not seek you. I want . . . ah! There he comes."

Kelly felt like laughing, but instead he swiveled himself around to look where the giant was looking. The compound was gone. In its stead was a hellish bath of burning debris and charges sputtering down to extinction. Smoke painted the darkness an oily gray. Through it came a man walking. A tall, thin man who moved with a grace of sinew and muscle all his own, a man who could glide without sound if he chose.

Kelly's mouth opened. His lips shaped 41's name. But he did not utter it aloud. He was dreaming, hallucinating, tweaking out beyond return.

But still the apparition came. Still it looked like 41, and as it drew nearer Kelly saw that it carried another. Long hair spilled over 41's arm and nearly swept the ground. Kelly stared, and without being aware of it he staggered to his feet.

An eddy of wind caught the embers and started a blaze near the former perimeter. The orange glow underlit 41's face, casting angles and shadows and turning his tawny eyes to molten brass. His long hair clung wet and dirty to his skull. His clothes were half-shredded, half-burned.

The giant beside Kelly grunted and shone his torch on 41, who ignored it. Without slackening step, 41 came to Kelly, the unconscious Cassandra cradled in his arms. And behind him, one supporting the other, came Caesar and Phila.

Kelly rubbed his eyes, wanting to believe them yet afraid to. 41 halted before him. His gaze bored into Kelly's, never wavering.

"I kept my promise," he said.

Kelly knew then that all of this was real. The blood seemed to drain through him, yet somehow he held himself up. "So did I," he said in a ghost of his usual voice. "Frant's dead."

Emotion flickered in 41's eyes. He started to smile, but did not. His head lifted. "Then it is over."

Kelly nodded although he did not quite understand. He gestured. "Thank you for bringing all of them out of there. How did you—"

"41," said the giant impatiently. "Time to go."

41 knelt and gently laid Cassandra upon the ground. Caesar was doubled over in a fit of coughing. Phila had crouched down wearily and was rubbing her face. All of them looked wonderful to Kelly. They had made it in spite of all the botches and hitches. They were all okay.

He watched 41 rise again and smiled at him. "Then are we back to—"

"I must go," said 41.

Disappointed, Kelly let his smile fade. "So I'm not forgiven?"

"There is nothing to forgive. This is another matter."

"I don't understand," said Kelly. "We can patch things up. I want you to stay in the Hawks. I need you. You're . . . you're my friend."

41's eyes clouded over. He looked down and kept his gaze there. He did not answer.

"Come!" said the giant. He added something else in the gutteral mercenary dialect.

Kelly could not exactly translate the term, but he knew it to be an insult. He waited for 41's explosion of anger. But it did not come. Instead, 41's shoulders hunched as though he had been lashed. He still did not look up.

"41," said Kelly in concern. "What is going on here? If our misunderstanding is cleared up, then we can fix this. Have you signed a contract with Harva Opie?"

41's head snapped up at that. "You know of this?"

"I know Opie's men when I see them," said Kelly. "That contract can be broken or renegotiated."

The giant laughed scornfully. "Not so," he said in heavily accented Glish. "You got the goods, 41. Now you pay for them."

"I must go," said 41 to Kelly.

But Kelly gripped his arm and would not let go. "What have you done? Tell me!"

Color flooded 41's face. "It was the only way to buy your life. It was the only way to bring you an army. It was the only way to defeat Frant and destroy this place."

"41—"

"You asked me once if I knew Frant. You asked me if I dealt. Yes, I knew Frant. But as a slave. I harvested rostma in these swamps many years ago. That is why I knew your plan would not work."

"You made it work," said Kelly softly. "But why the hell didn't you tell me this before we started? You could have explained—"

"No. Your mind was set." This time 41 did smile, although briefly. "You see, I know you well. Goodbye, Kelly."

He held out his hand. Kelly stared at him, emotions grabbing his throat so that he could not speak. He knew how much 41 hated a handshake. He understood now what it meant as he gripped 41's calloused palm.

They would not see each other again.

The lump in Kelly's throat grew. He couldn't let it happen. Yet the giant stood there—red-eyed, cyborged, armored. And 41 was walking away, not looking back, his head bowed submissively. For the first time since Kelly had met him, he saw the slave that 41 had once been.

It tore at him. Kelly took a step after them. "41!"

41 paused and glanced back, but the giant seized the back of

his neck and thrust him onward. The dark jungle swallowed them, with only a golden bob of the torch to mark their passage. Then the light faded from sight as well, and they were gone.

"Boss?"

Kelly turned, still trying to come to grips with it. "Yes, Caesar?"

"What was all of that about? Who were those goons he brought?"

"Some of the best-trained, worst-feared mercenaries in the galaxy," said Kelly thoughtfully. "What the devil kind of bargain has he made with them? He can't go back to being a slave again. He's been free too long. It would kill him. And they'll never trust him as a soldier."

"You mean," said Caesar slowly, his voice hoarse from smoke inhalation, "that he did all this for us? Just us?"

Kelly nodded. He was ashamed now of his anger and suspicion, ashamed of the accusations he had flung at 41 earlier.

"Well," said Caesar. "What do we do now?"

It was a good question. Kelly was too numb to battle their situation any longer. He struggled to hold himself together just a few minutes more.

"We thank God we're all still alive," he said first. "Then we get back to the *Sabre* and sleep for a year. Then we make our report to headquarters and deliver the ambassador back to her people. Then we go after 41."

"To hunt him down?"

"No. To get him back. He saved our butts, Caesar. And we're not going to thank him by leaving him in Harva Opie's hands."

Caesar stared and even Phila looked up.

"Yusus, Boss. We can't take on a whole army."

"Yes, we can," said Kelly. "And we will. The Hawks don't leave their own behind."

He knelt beside Cassandra and gently smoothed her hair from her face. He made his prayer, then he called Siggerson.

"This is the *Sabre*," said Siggerson promptly, sounding worried. "What's going on? You were cut off. Was I supposed to pick you up?"

"Not then," said Kelly. "You are now. We need four wristbands first."

"Only four? But there are—"

"The ambassador's staff didn't make it," said Kelly.

"Anyone else hurt or not coming back?" asked Siggerson.

"Beaulieu and the ambassador are both injured. Have gurneys waiting in the teleport bay. As for 41—"

"41! Commander, he jumped ship and is—"

"I know," said Kelly gently. "41 will be coming home . . . later."

Breaking contact, Kelly gazed down at Cassandra in the darkness. The moons were now shining down.

Was she worth all this?

Kelly smiled to himself.

Yes.